The floating city was a gorgeous vision as they approached it across the luminous sea. Some of the wicker structures were painted in gay and gaudy profusion of colors that ranged from rose-pink to carnation and vermillion, pale blue, rich greens, indigo, lavender, tangerine—a dazzling variety of colors that made the incredible place look like an elfin city in a fairytale.

Flags and banners and pennons fluttered from rooftops and gateposts and masts. Silken carpets or tapestries hung from every aperture.

An insubstantial town of Faerie, floating like a mirage on an unknown sea beneath the world . . .

. . . Where Alph the sacred river ran
Through caverns measureless to man,
Down to a sunless sea.

—*Samuel Taylor Coleridge*

DOWN TO A
SUNLESS SEA

Lin Carter

DAW BOOKS, INC.

DONALD A. WOLLHEIM, PUBLISHER

1633 Broadway, New York, NY 10019

To my friend
Robert M. Price,
editor of *Crypt of Cthulhu*.

First Printing, June 1984
1 2 3 4 5 6 7 8 9

DAW TRADEMARK REGISTERED
U.S. PAT. OFF. MARCA
REGISTRADA. HECHO EN U.S.A.

PRINTED IN U.S.A.

I

THE STRANGERS

1
The Storm

When Brant saw the sooty smudge on the horizon, he reined in his loper with a muttered curse and sat the saddle, staring with narrowed eyes.

Dust storms are very rare on Mars, where the bitter-cold air is too thin to maintain dust particles for long. But air, however thin, remains air and has its currents.

And that dark, bruise-purple blur on the skyline was a dust storm, all right.

He growled another curse, and felt despair gnaw at his heart. He was a big, hard man with a dark, strong face and eyes as fiery black as Satan's heart. Not a man to have very often known fear.

Well, he knew it now. . . .

The thick, thick dust that carpets the dead sea bottoms of Mars is fine as talcum. It seeps into the pores of your skin, it leaks through solid plastic, even through a thermal suit of nioflex. There is no way to keep it out of your eyes, your lungs, your guts. And that is under ordinary conditions . . . but when ten thousand tons of superfine particles come howling down on you, whipping and whirling on every side. . . .

It's not a slow death, true. But it's not an easy death, either.

He rose in the saddle and looked around, using his UV goggles, for day was dimming toward the sudden nightfall of this far world and it was hard to see for any great distance. Everywhere, save to the south, he saw gaunt-ribbed plains of empty rock, for he was atop one of the stony plateaus that had been ancient continents once, lush and fertile, lifting sheer from the seething waves of prehistoric seas. It was either that, ride the highline, as they called it, or waste your loper's strength slogging through the tenacious dust that pulled and sucked like a lake of molasses.

When the oceans dried up and the living things dwindled, the continents had cracked like an apple skin drying in the sun. Some of these fissures were dozens of fathoms deep . . . but none of them afforded him a safe haven from the hissing storm that was approaching.

Brant had gone riding out from Sun Lake City a month before, angling south across the great stony continent called Ogygis Regio. He wasn't looking for anything in particular; he wasn't even prospecting. But there was a corpse back in the city with a knife in its guts, and the handle had his fingerprints all over it. The Colonial Administration cops were a philosophical lot, and another barroom brawl was just another barroom brawl. It would all blow over in time, Brant knew, but for a while it would be healthy not to be around.

Well, when that crawling stain of dark purple spreading across the sky got here, he would be neither healthy nor around. Again, he searched the bleak terrain for a hiding place, but saw nothing. Nothing but . . . what was that huddle of jumbled rock to the south? He turned up the frequency on his goggles and peered again.

Excitement flared within Brant, for it was a city. The ruins of one, rather. When all this gaunt plateau had been lush with leafage, it had been a proud and princely metropolis, perhaps. Now it was dead as Nineveh and Tyre, although much, much older.

He pulled the reptile's head around and thumped bootheels in its scaly sides. It voiced a shrill hiss of displeasure, then broke into that clumsy gait for which it was named.

With luck, he might barely reach a place of refuge in the ruins, before the wings of the storm closed around him. Anything would do, a crypt, a cellar, a mausoleum.

Anything was better than the soft, clinging tomb he feared, buried alive beneath tons of hissing cinnamon-colored dust.

*   *   *

He made the walls well before the storm swept down upon him. There was no need to find the gates, for the walls had fallen a million years ago, and lay tumbled about, huge untidy slabs, like a game of dominoes abandoned by the careless children of giants. He rode into streets older than Egypt and past the hollow shells of palaces that were young before the first man-things crept whimpering from the steaming fens under the nodding cycads of a forgotten Dawn.

All of pale golden marble and rose-pink stone was the city built. It had been fair once, very fair. Like an ancient crone who had once been famous for her loveliness, the bones of its lost, faded beauty still showed, here and there.

Forlorn and ruined, it was still a dream of fairness with its pale golden marble and old pink stone, dreaming under the purple sky. And a line from an old, old poem whispered from the depths of his memory—

A rose-red city, half as old as time.

He rode his loper into a square that had been ancient before the cornerstones of the first pyramid were hewn and set in place beside the green Nile, and here he found the first of many mysteries.

They had staked the woman out to die.

They had stripped her mother-naked and tied her wrists and ankles with tight, cruel thongs to pegs driven deep into the crevices between the ancient flagstones.

She was not yet dead, although her tongue protruded, swollen, between parched, cracked lips and black circles of fatigue were drawn around her lustrous eyes.

Nor had her suffering dimmed the bright, fierce spirit of her, for she raised her dust-dark face from the flags to glare at him in silent menace. *Does she think I'm going to rape her?* thought Brant wryly.

It wasn't a bad idea, at that, for she was very beautiful, with the long, supple legs of a dancer, a narrow waist, and high, proud, full, yet pointed, breasts.

He dismounted, cast a wary glance behind him at the darkening sky, and strode to where she lay spread-eagled.

He gave her water, just a dribble at first, to moisten her lips and tongue slightly. She sucked greedily at each drop as if her life depended on it, which, of course, it did. Then a little more.

She essayed a question, but her voice was an unintelligible croak. He shook his head, gave her a few drops more. Then he took out his knife and cut the thongs, prying them from the tender flesh of her swollen wrists and feet. Tenderly, he began to chafe the circulation back into her limbs. Like all of the natives, she had the coppery-red skin and russet hair and lambent emerald eyes he was accustomed to. But whereas most of the Martian women straighten their wooly hair into long and lustrous tresses, usually dyed ink-black, she wore her furcap short and trimmed like that of a man. It gave her a piquant, gamine appeal he found stirring.

From the looks of her, she had been here three days, perhaps longer. It was a marvel that she still lived, the copper-red woman with the emerald eyes. But she was of the Low Clans, surely, and they are tough and strong.

Tough, and hard to kill. His lips twisted in a dour grin that bared white teeth. They have to be that way, the Martian natives of the wild nomad clans, for the Colonial Administration has done everything they could have done to ensure they did not survive.

He gave the naked women more water, and she drank it gratefully. But her eyes were still cold and wary, filled with menace, fiery with contempt and hatred. To her he was only a cursed *f'yagh*, an Outworlder from nearer the sun, come to loot and plunder her dying planet of its last pitiful treasures.

Brant dug into his loose robes for the brandy, but the woman stopped him with a curt nod.

"I am strong enough . . . see to her, to my 'sister' . . ."

He looked and saw, under a crumbling portico, yet another naked woman staked out to die like the first. And his dark brow scowled with puzzlement: what crime had these women done, to merit such a cruel, slow, lingering death?

He went to tend to the second as he had the first. There was no menace in her doe-soft eyes, only dim bewilderment and stirrings of fear. Where the first woman had been lithe and lean, the second was soft and rounded, a timid little woman to be coddled and cuddled—as for the first, Brant would rather cuddle a sandcat.

By the time he had gotten both women to their feet, the storm was upon them, shrilling like a thousand demons, sheets of dark red sand hissing between the pillars. Brant loosed the loper, let it precede him into the interior of the nearest building while he half-carried and half-dragged the two women to shelter. The tall one with the dancer's legs shouldered him aside, to take the smaller one in her arms, hands locked under soft, plump breasts.

"Okay then, do it yourself," growled Brant under his breath. But he loosened the power gun in its worn holster on his thigh. *That* one would as lief put a knife between his ribs as look at him, water-sharing or no water-sharing.

They sought refuge in the cellars, which were as bone dry as most of Mars. Crouched in the gloom, they heard the weird, high song of the dust screaming by overhead.

He unlimbered the saddlebags and took out a squat little cooker powered by dialectric accumulators, and began warming up food. It wasn't much of a meal, beef stew and canned beans, but all three devoured it hungrily, although the women wrinkled up their noses suspiciously at the odd, foreign smell and taste of it.

He gave them brandy mixed with water, got up, took out his sleeping bag and strode to the corner of the cellar that was the farthest from where the two women sat, and made his bed for the night. Then he tended to the loper's needs, giving it dried plant-fiber cakes in a leather sack and a few plump leaves and stems for the moisture they contained. Like earthly camels, the ungainly reptiles needed little water and that seldom, but they did need some. Replete, the reptile curled up like a huge dog in a corner, and slept.

And then Brant sought his own rest. Greatly daring, he rolled over and turned his back upon the women, leaving them to their own devices.

In a while, the tall one got up to rummage through the loper's saddlebags. She found loose robes of warm cloth, and she and her "sister" curled up together, wrapped in the robes against the night's chill.

Brant lay awake and wary a long time, waiting, but nothing chanced.

After a time, he slept.

His gun had been in his hand all the while.

Above them, the storm-wind shrilled like a flock of banshees.

But after a time, the storm slept, too.

2
The Women

With dawn he woke to delicious odors and rose to find that the tall woman had arisen before him, and had heated the remnants of last night's meal, pouring equal portions into three ceramic bowls she had found God-knows-where.

She and her plump "sister" squatted on their heels, wrapped in the clinging robes they had discovered in the saddlebags, wordlessly waiting for him to join them and to share the meagre meal.

It was a gesture of peace, he knew. He flashed them a hard grin and went to sit across from them, squatting as easily as did they. And they ate together, and "shared water."

That little ritual was very important. There was water-truce between them now, he knew; neither would violate the unspoken truce unless he attempted to harm them, or tried to take them by force.

The ritual done, Brant addressed them, laying his hand upon his hard-muscled chest and speaking his name carefully.

The women frowned slightly at the odd name, but the tall one laid her long-fingered hand between her thrusting breasts and said in the ancient speech, "I am Zuarra; this is my 'sister,' Suoli." Her speech had the tang of the Low Clans in it, he noticed. And again he wondered for what sin they had been staked out by their people to die, but knew better than to offend Custom by daring to ask.

He nodded, finished the last drop of his meal, then rose.

"Best that we get started," he said gruffly. "We may have to dig ourselves out of here."

The storm had passed overhead sometime during the night, and the dawn sky was clear. Fine dust squeaked and crunched grittily underfoot as they emerged onto the square and looked about them, grateful to be alive.

While he was saddling the loper, the taller woman approached him.

"Whither do you go, O Brant?" she inquired.

He shrugged good-humoredly. "Nowhere in particular, girl. Where do you want to go? I guess you will not be returning to the camps of your people?" It was really not intended as a question, nor did she take it for one.

"The Moon Hawk nation are our people no longer," she said without inflection. Then, with a little cold smile that bared sharp teeth in an ugly grimace, she added: "Suoli, my 'sister,' says we should go to the city of the *f'yagh*, there to open our thighs to your kind for bread and meat."

Brant said nothing, but grinned inwardly. The Earthsider colonist who tried to bed this wench would find a knife between his ribs before he got her thighs apart, he knew. But, after all, what else was there for the two women to do? It is hard enough for a man, even a warrior, to be *aoudh*—an outcast. It was even harder for a woman.

But he was not going back to the colony at Solis Lacus yet, not for another month, at least, and he said as much. And there was not another Earthsider colony in these southerly parts between here and the Pole.

Zuarra took the news stolidly.

"We will cook for you and clean for you and gather plants for water, and guard you while you sleep," she said in her husky, deep-throated voice. "But we will not open our thighs for you, neither my 'sister' nor myself."

Brant felt his temper rise at that cold, flat, level statement. He had been too long without a woman, and this one was damnably attractive in a lean, boyish sort of way. But he had his pride, too, and it was as fierce as was Zuarra's.

"I have not asked you to," he grated, meeting her eye to eye. "Nor shall I."

"Then we understand each other, O Brant," she said

tonelessly. He nodded, and turned his back to finish saddling the reptile.

The last thing he needed was to have two helpless women on his hands, and women, too, that he could not go to bed with. But he clamped his lips over a growled curse. What could he do? He couldn't just leave them here to die.

His had been a hard life, had Brant's, since the courts sent him to Mars, to the penal colony at Trivium Charontis. Since working his way to freedom, he had run guns to the High Clan princes, and sold them liquor and forbidden tobacco, and peddled narcotics to the soft, timid Earthsider clerks and stenographers. He had killed a man more than once; he had cheated at cards; he had stolen.

But he had never treated a woman harshly or unjustly. It was not in him, for a certain rude chivalry flickered in his soul.

He would not betray the best that was within him now.

They rode east, into the Argyre, with the women taking turns in the saddle while he plodded along, leading the loper.

He had no way of knowing it, but he had already taken the first few steps toward the most fantastic adventure any man had ever lived. . . .

The sky above them was clear, grape-purple, with a few long, thin ribbons of pink cloud-vapor high and to the west. The sun was a small, dull, hard disc of yellow-white fire to the east.

They kept to the high country, to the top of the level rock plateau, with Suoli riding astride the loper, as she was the weakest of the three. Brant and Zuarra strode afoot, alternately leading the reptile by the loop of the reins.

After a time, the loose robe entangling her legs, making her stumble, she swore, removed the garment, and went forward naked. Brant dropped back behind her a little, admiring her long-legged, tireless stride and watching the roll of her firm buttocks as she led the way.

She was damnably desirable, and in the beauty of her nakedness she struck fire in his loins. But he neither said nor did aught to let her know it. He had enough trouble on his hands just then, without aggravating this tawny wildcat of a woman.

After some hours, they came to a deep, narrow ravine in the level tableland, where fat-leaved plants grew. These the women gathered for the pressure-still, while Brant clambered from ledge to ledge, hunting. Erelong, he found a fat, tangerine-colored reptile whose flesh he knew from experience to be edible, and slew it with a bolt from his power gun, the dial set to needle-beam.

While the women skinned and disemboweled the kill, Brant searched the Colonial Administration Survey charts he carried to seek some sort of haven against the bitter cold of night. They could not be lucky enough to find another dead city, he knew, and this was dangerous country. Predatory reptiles called rock dragons made their lairs in crevices such as these. Customarily, they hunted and fed on the same sort of plump, harmless lizards as the one Brant had just slain; but they were not averse to the taste of manflesh, either.

They rested for a time, and Brant fed more plant fiber to the loper, while the women cooked the steaks and chops they had trimmed from the carcass of the lizard in the portable cooker. That night they would feast, he knew.

He stood and watched them as they worked together, squatting on their heels, hands moving with practiced skill, and he wondered what their story might be.

It had not been for naught that two such women, young, each attractive in different ways, both of child-bearing age, had been staked out to die a slow, lingering death from thirst and starvation, he knew.

But he also knew better than to ask.

They rode on, as the distant sun declined in the west and the sky darkened to deep purple. Brant had found a haven on the Survey map, a mound of broken rocks believed to have been the burial mound of an ancient king, since it was obviously of artificial origin. When they reached it by late afternoon or early evening, he unpacked the small tents of heat-retaining plastic he had brought along for himself and the loper in case they rode into the polar wastes. One of these he set up for himself, the other for the women. The loper he tethered to a boulder, and fed the creature on the remainder of the fibre.

They shared the meal, seated on opposite sides of the fire. It was not wood they burned, of course, since Mars has nothing in the way of trees, but a colorless, aromatic oil in a flat pan. This fluid provided both warmth and light.

The fresh-cooked meat tasted good, after a diet of canned goods. The steaks were succulent and juicy and broiled to perfection. But when he complimented Zuarra on her culinary skills, she shot him a level, contemptuous glance and her mouth twisted sardonically, saying nothing. It was as if, by praising her skills as a woman, he had somehow insulted her.

Brant shrugged irritably, and devoured his meat. Let them have their secrets, he thought to himself.

The sky darkened and became ablaze with stars. These were bright, hard, unwinking, unlike the stars that shone in earthly skies, because the air of Mars is thin.

It became distinctly colder, and the women donned their borrowed robes.

Before long, they sought their tents, but not to sleep, as it chanced.

Brant tossed and turned in his bedroll. Although the long day's journey had wearied him, his mind was too active for him to fall asleep easily.

After a time, feeling the need to relieve himself, he rose, unseamed the tent, and crawled out under the stars.

Seeking a crevice into which to urinate, he chanced to pass the tent wherein the women lay. And as he approached he heard odd sounds from within—whispers, moans, gasping sighs.

Curious, he peered through the transparent panel, and the sight that met his eyes made his mouth twist in a cold, wolfish grin. The nude limbs mingling, the hands searching, the wet mouths hungrily feasting, the warm bodies intertwined. . . .

Now he knew the crime for which the two had been staked out to die in such a cruel manner. The sin, rather: for to the

High Law the love they shared was deemed unnatural and perverse.

Now he understood the peculiar emphasis which Zuarra placed on the word "sister." He should have guessed it before, but had thought little of it. Well, returning to his tent, now at least he knew exactly why neither of the two wished to "open their thighs" to him.

Oddly enough, he fell asleep instantly, and slept a deep and dreamless sleep till dawn.

3

The Dragon

They broke their fast that next morning with a frugal meal, for Brant was anxious to conserve the food supplies that remained to them. He could not know when he next would make a kill, for the plateau was bleak and inhospitable to life in any form.

They moved on, ever south, then angling east, for it seemed to Brant that there was a greater chance of finding game on the crumbling edges of the ancient continent, where plants and lizards thrived in the crevices of the cliff.

The women made no objection to this plan, so they went on as they had done the day before, with weak little Suoli riding in the saddle while Brant and Zuarra walked afoot.

Very few words were exchanged between them. Brant was in a surly mood, and neither of the women felt overly communicative. From time to time, as they walked together, Zuarra stole a sidewise glance out of her emerald eyes at the tall Earthsider, but sensed his dour mood, and addressed him seldom.

From time to time, during rest halts, Brant consulted the Survey map. He heartily disliked a journey like this, that had no clear or definite destination. The farther they wandered into the south, the colder and more barren the land would become. They would have ever increasing difficulty in finding the fat-leafed, knee-high plants that, cooked in the pressure still, would provide them with water and with fodder for the beast.

There was no colony between here and the pole, he knew,

19

and even if they were to chance upon an encampment of the People, they would be as hostile to one of the accursed *f'yagh* as they would to the two outlawed women who rode with him.

A cave in the cliffside, however, would afford them shelter and a certain measure of security. With such a place as their base of operations, he and the women could venture forth to forage for water-plants and for game.

They rode on, into the east.

It was like riding to the edge of the world, the emptiness, the vast and cloudless sky above, where no birds flew. The rocky plateau was sterile and featureless, scoured by the fine sand the wind stirred. There were no vivid colors to break the eye-aching monotony of dull purple sky, dark stone, cinnamon sand. There were no sounds to speak of to relieve the dead silence, just the creak of saddle leather, the padding of the loper's splayed feet, the faint, far moaning of a weary wind.

The women felt it too, and grew restless and uneasy at the silence and the dead land over which they plodded. After a time, little Suoli whimpered plaintively that she was weary of riding in the saddle and that its hard leather was chafing her raw.

"I would rather walk for a time," she whined. Brant shrugged and helped her down. When he offered the seat to the tall woman, she refused it curtly, so Brant climbed astride the beast himself and rode awhile, watching the two women narrowly as they walked along together, side by side, whispering to each other in tones too faint for him to distinguish.

It was a relief to ride in relative comfort after so long afoot. The muscles of calf and thigh ached with fatigue, and the swaying gait of the reptile was comforting. After a little while, Brant dozed, retaining his seat with the automatic responses of one who has spent years in the saddle. The women did not disturb his brief rest, talking in low voices to each other.

Suddenly, Suoli shrilled, pointing into the east, and Brant snapped out of his doze, clawing his power gun from its worn holster. Then he relaxed, muttering a curse, for it was only one of the moons that the little woman had spied low in the sky near the horizon.

He grinned, though. In truth, the twin moons of Mars were a rare sight to see and you could go a year or more without ever glimpsing Deimos or Phobos. The reason for this was simple, for, although both moons ride closer to the surface of their primary than does Earth's satellite, they have a very low albedo—so low as to render them virtually invisible to the eye most of the time. You have to know precisely where to look—and when—in order to see them at all, except by accident.

Now that Suoli's cry of delight and surprise had roused him from his rest, he offered the saddle to Zuarra, but she dismissed the gesture impatiently.

"Ride on and rest further, O Brant," she said in clipped tones. "You are weary, but I am young and strong." Was there a trace of scorn in her voice? Brant shrugged, caring little.

Both women walked wrapped in the burnous-like robes, he noticed, for the air was chill here at the edges of the plateau, bitterly cold, from the air currents which came across the antarctic barrens from the southern pole. Brant thumbed the dial of his heated suit to a higher setting.

In another hour they had come to the very edge of the ancient continent. Here the dry rock was cloven asunder by a thousand narrow crevices, and the footing was treacherous with loose rock. He dismounted and led the loper forward cautiously, testing his footing every few steps.

The problem was, simply, how to get down to the dead sea bottom? They were a hundred yards above the level plains of the dustlands, and a loper is bad at climbing. For a time they skirted the brink, looking for safe ways of descent, and at length they discovered that for which Brant had been watchful—a series of crumbling ledges of rock strata, like a great stair.

They began going down, taking great care, guiding the

loper, who hissed and squealed with alarm, not liking the descent very much.

Zuarra clambered down on lithe and limber legs, with the agility of an acrobat, assisting the nervous Suoli from ledge to ledge, while Brant and the loper took up the rear.

He led the restive beast down, cautious step after cautious step, wary of the treacherous ground under his boot heels. Once, eons before, this had been the continental shelf, washed by the waves of one of the lost, age-forgotten oceans of primal Mars. Here and there, between the mineral outcroppings, the Earthsider spied fossil shells, strange and unearthly in their shapings, but unmistakable.

He wondered briefly if, a billion years from now, the seas of his distant homeworld would dry to sterile deserts, and the shores of Europe and Africa and the two Americas would resemble this crumbling, time-eroded cliff. . . .

Shortly thereafter, Suoli *screamed*. There was stark terror in her tones, that were very unlike the cry of pleasure with which she had greeted her rare glimpse of the hurtling moon.

Brant had his back turned to the dustlands and was trying to urge the reluctant reptile down from one broken ledge to another, when that shrill cry rang out. Growling a startled curse, he tried to turn, but thin plates of rock broke beneath him and he came down on his backside and would have perhaps fallen farther had not his hand been tangled in the loper's reins.

The stubborn reptile planted its forefeet firmly, and in so doing, broke Brant's impending tumble into the abyss.

Struggling to free his gun-hand from the tight reins, Brant looked beneath him . . . and the marrow froze in his bones at the sight that met his gaze.

Wriggling from its hidden lair between two ledges of rock strata, a hideous form emerged to their view.

It was the dreaded rock dragon; he should have known this tier of crumbling ledges made a perfect hiding place for the deadly reptiles.

It must have measured fifteen feet from fanged, gaping maw to wriggling, barbed tail. Its scaly length—the middle parts as big around as the Earthsider's upper thigh—was mailed in thick, overlapping scales of the same dull, liver-color as the rocks amidst which it made its home.

Zuarra was directly in its path.

As for Suoli, the frightened girl cowered on the far corner of the ledge, uttering piercing squeals, fluttering her plump little hands foolishly at the serpent, as if hoping to shoo it away.

It was not a true serpent, the rock dragon, for while its slithering length was serpentine, three sets of short, bowed legs, armed with birdlike claws, sprouted at even intervals down its length.

Zuarra was frozen, facing the deadly thing. And her hands were empty of weapons.

Sharp claws clutching and closing upon the thin ledge, squealing under its fierce clench, the dragon reared above her, jaws agape. Its jaws bore retractable fangs, hollow like hypodermic needles, and as the dragon extruded them into view, all three of the travelers saw the oily, colorless fluid that dribbled out.

The bite of a rock dragon contains no poisonous venom, true; but those fangs inject into living flesh a substance that causes instantaneous paralysis. Once those fangs closed upon Zuarra, she would be helpless to resist while the mud-colored thing wound a loop of its scaly length about her torso, to drag her down into its hole to be devoured at leisure.

And Brant could not free his wrist from the entangling reins.

4

The Gun

While Brant struggled to free his wrist from the reins, Zuarra cast a quick glance about her in desperation, seeking some weapon wherewith to defend herself. But nothing met her gaze that could help battle against the rock dragon.

She turned an imploring look at her "sister," who cowered whimpering in the far corner of the ledge, and cried out to her for help. But the soft little woman only buried her face in her hands, ignoring Zuarra's plea for assistance.

The six-legged serpent had crawled entirely out of its burrow by this time, and reared above the helpless woman, fanged and drooling jaws agape, seeming to savor the feast of warm flesh that stood so temptingly near. One set of clawed feet clutched the rocky ledge, the two other sets opened and closed on empty air, claws clashing together with a rasping, ugly sound that made both women shudder.

Then it bent its hideous head down toward its fear-frozen victim, its lithe and serpentine body curving into the shape of the letter "S."

The dripping fangs were fully extruded from the gums by now. Within more moments, those clutching claws would close upon Zuarra—the huge serpent would whip one coil of its long, wriggling body about her, and the fangs would sink into her throat or breast. Then there would be nothingness for the tall woman, a rapidly spreading numbness sucking her down into a bottomless well of darkness. . . .

The horrible jaws bent nearer and nearer to her face. Time seemed to slow down to an agonizing crawl. The limits of the world shrank until only she and the rock dragon existed. Oddly, Zuarra had never felt so thoroughly alive before: the blood sang through her veins, the cinnamon expanse of the desert bore an indescribably gorgeous coloration, the air was sweet and cool in her nostrils.

It seemed to the woman that she was simultaneously aware of every muscle and sinew and tendon in her body. Every cell and nerve and tissue of her body tingled with vitality. Her heart beat desperately against her ribs like a trapped bird fighting against the bars of its narrow cage.

What thoughts or memories flashed through her seething brain in that endless infinity of a moment, she could never afterward recall.

Brant strove, but could not free his gun hand. But with the left hand he clawed free the second pistol from its holster at his other hip and tossed it to where Suoli cowered whimpering.

"Catch, girl—!" he bawled.

But she only flinched and squealed, burying her frightened face in her hands as the power gun skidded across the ledge and went clattering over the brink, well out of reach.

Zuarra saw it all with that total clarity of vision that comes in the moments of greatest peril. But she could not move, frozen with fear.

Time slowed to a stop. The world hung breathless, as if waiting.

Then—

"Down on your face, girl!"

The hoarse shout seemed to come to her ears from an immense distance. She puzzled slowly over the meaning of the words, and then, her will frozen into a mindless state like a tranced dream, she complied, kneeling on the edge of the shelf of strata, like an acolyte prostrating herself before a monstrous idol.

The dim shadows that veiled this portion of the cliff split apart—cloven asunder by a fierce spear of intolerable fire.

Suoli squeaked fearfully, and tried to crawl into the solid rock of the cliff to hide herself.

The bolt caught the dragon directly between its open jaws.

Its ugly head literally exploded in a flying splatter of burnt bone and crisped gobbets of meat.

Oily black gore fountained into the air from the stump of its neck. Claws clutched spasmodically on the lip of the ledge, the hard stone squeaking under their pressure.

Slowly the serpentine body bent backwards over the abyss. The claws lost their hold, and the twitching body, coiling and uncoiling slowly, toppled from the ledge to thud into the loose rocks at the bottom of the cliff.

And it was all over. . . .

Unable to free his wrist from the twisted reins of the loper, Brant had awkwardly fumbled his second power gun from its holster, aimed it clumsily with his left hand, and fired, snapping off a shot aimed by sheer instinct alone, as time was running out.

The dial which adjusted the width of the beam was still set to the narrowest aperture—the needle-beam setting to which he had adjusted the weapon when he had used it yesterday, hunting lizards for meat.

This meant, of course, that the shot would have to be a direct hit, which was risky. But the urgency of the situation was such that there was certainly no time for him to try to thumb the dial to a wider beam setting.

Fortunately—for Zuarra—he was a dead shot, even with his left hand.

The woman knelt, stunned and shaking, where she had crouched in mindless obedience to his shouted command. She seemed oblivious to her surroundings.

Eventually, Brant got his hand free, returned the power gun to its holster, and clambered down to the ledge where the two native women were.

He put his arm around Zuarra and raised her to her feet. She cowered against him, hiding her face against his breast. He patted her trembling shoulder, speaking gently to her as one comforts a frightened child.

Erelong, the whiteness left her face and her eyes took on an expression of awareness. Still in his arms, and clinging to him for support, since her knees were rubbery and her legs seemed nerveless, she looked at Suoli with an expression of icy contempt.

Before that scathing expression, the soft little woman flushed, dropped her own gaze, and bit her full lower lip in vexation.

"Are you all right, girl?" asked Brant urgently.

The Martian woman met his searching gaze.

"I am unharmed, O Brant," she whispered tonelessly. And then, a moment later, she added:

"It was well for Zuarra that you fired your *f'yagha* weapon when you did."

He nodded, with a rare smile lightening his usually dour, grim expression. Then, half carrying and half dragging her, he took her to a place of safety at the back of the ledge, and helped her to sit, offering her water, which she drank greedily.

They rested for a time, saying nothing. Eventually, little Suoli came to join them. She reached out one timid hand to touch Zuarra, but the other woman jerked her arm away, not even looking at her friend.

Brant said nothing, but observed it all narrowly.

The harsh, whistling cry of the loper still stranded on the ledge above them roused the Earthsider to a remembrance of their situation.

Night would soon be upon the world, and the cliffside was dangerous enough by day; it would be perilous to attempt to negotiate it under conditions of darkness. And there might well be other rock dragons coiled waiting in their lairs beneath the shelves of stony strata.

"Do you feel steady enough to continue climbing down?" he inquired. Zuarra got to her feet and made that Martian gesture which was the native equivalent of a nod.

Leaving the women to climb down by themselves, Brant went back up to the ledge where the loper stood, crying plaintively, and began again to guide it down the stairlike shelves of stone.

Night had long since come down, dark-winged, over the world by the time the three of them and the beast reached the bottom of the cliff at last, and Brant searched for and retrieved the pistol that he had tossed toward Suoli.

Fastidiously avoiding the cadaver of the rock dragon—which still writhed in the slow undulations of its death-spasms, the two women gathered fat, water-bearing leaves from the plants which grew thickly in the shelter of the cliff and fed them into the pressure still, while Brant erected the two tents and fed the loper its dinner of plant fiber.

They lit a fire in the flat pan and shared the remaining meat from yesterday's kill between them. The women did not speak and Brant remained silent. From time to time, Suoli stole a shy glance at her companion, who ignored her presence as if she did not even exist.

Brant set up precautions against the dangers that he knew were all too present. This close to the crumbling side of the cliff there could well be many nests of rock dragons, so he unlimbered a protective fence made of aluminum pegs and a single strand of wire attached to a small dialectric accumulator. If anything touched the low fence during the night, it would suffer an electrical shock which should be sufficiently painful to drive off even the hungriest predator.

Fortunately, they did not have to worry about sandcats this close to the cliff, as those dreaded beasts preferred the vast expanses of the dustlands where they were wont to tunnel subterranean lairs.

The women went to their tent, but Brant lingered by the firepan, too bone-weary for slumber.

He heard low voices in conversation. Words rose to an angry pitch. There came the sound of a ringing slap and Suoli's shrill squeak of pain.

Thereafter, the voices subsided.

Brant grinned wolfishly, and sought his own tent.

With dawn they rose from rest, and Brant observed, but made no comment upon the fact, that Suoli seemed more cowed and subdued than was usual.

She also had an ugly, purplish bruise beneath one eye.

Zuarra met his eyes flatly, but said nothing about the events of the night.

Brant saddled up the loper, struck the tents, and recoiled his protective fence into its niche in the saddlebags.

They rode on into the morning.

5

The Strangers

All that morning they rode along the clifflike edge of the ancient continent, where the loose rocks and debris made their footing far easier than the talcum-fine sands of the dustland would have afforded them.

Brant was looking for a deep, capacious cave in the cliffwall, one that would give them the ultimate protection from beasts and inclement weather. And, preferably, a cave that was not already occupied by one of the dangerous predators that abound on Mars.

The three of them took turns riding in the saddle, and this time Zuarra did not yield her turn to Suoli, who was therefore made to plod wearily along on foot as often as her companions. The weak little woman whined and snuffled a little at this lack of preferential treatment, but to her protestations Zuarra paid no attention, her face set in grim mien.

The big Earthsider made no comment and ignored the rift between the two women. *A lover's spat,* he thought to himself sardonically.

Along toward midday, with the sun a cold ball of pale flame at the meridian, Brant was jolted from his lethargy when the loper suddenly lifted its head and sniffed at the cold air with its scaly snout high. It then gave voice to a harsh cry, almost a challenge.

"What is it, O Brant?" asked Zuarra, scanning the vicinity with alert gaze. The Earthsider shrugged; but something had definitely aroused the loper's vigilance and, from the direction in which it craned its long, snaky neck, the source of the reptile's discomfiture seemed to be out in the midst of the dustlands.

Brant was an old Mars hand, and knew that the deadly sandcat makes it lair, tunneled beneath the fine dust of the deserts, lying in wait to trap the unwary, who tread upon the thin surface of its hiding place, break through, and provide the predator with fresh meat. But something in the behavior of the loper made him think it had detected some other form of life than a sandcat.

He wondered what it might be. Then he unlimbered his pair of binoculars from the saddlebags and began to search the dreary flatness of the dustland.

The powerful lenses had been adapted to the dimmer daylight of the Red Planet, and could be adjusted to various degrees of distance. By their aid he soon ascertained the cause of the loper's fretfulness.

"What have you seen, O Brant?" demanded Zuarra breathlessly.

"Strangers," he said briefly. "Two of them, at least. In trouble of some sort."

"Let us go on," suggested nervous little Suoli in a timid voice, "and leave them to their problem, which is not ours."

Brant grunted, saying nothing, but Zuarra shot her "sister" a scathing glance of pure contempt. Survival is a deadly struggle in the great dustlands of Mars, and even clan-war and blood-feud are ignored when strangers meet.

"Wait here," he said tersely, mounting the loper and turning its head out into the desert.

"We will go with you," said Zuarra, "to share together what may chance to befall." Behind her words was the obvious fact that, without Brant and the loper, they would have no chance to live very long in this desolate and hostile region.

"Suit yourself," Brant said flatly. "But keep up!"

They made slow progress in the thick, soft sands, which sucked at their feet like quicksand and impeded every stride. However, Zuarra made no complaint and little Suoli dared not even whimper.

The loper, with its flat, splay-footed stride, moved more quickly and easily atop the superfine sands than did the two women; however, an extended journey across the dustland would soon exhaust it, as well.

Brant was not overly familiar with these Argyre dustlands, except that he was aware that they were vast in expanse and were cleft in twain by a very deep but very narrow canyon called the Erebus—one of those lesions in the rocky crust made eons ago when the planet dried and cracked and shrunk with the loss of its ancient oceans.

He hoped they would not have to travel as far as the canyon to reach the imperiled strangers, but doubted they could be that far off. Had they been, he did not think it possible for the loper to have scented them in the distance.

Fortunately, the newcomers were on this side of the Erebus, and not as far off as he had feared. Only a few minutes of hard riding brought Brant a closer view of them.

There were two men and two riding-beasts, and one of the lopers was clearly dead, the victim of a sandcat's attack, from the clawed and torn condition of its carcass. Indeed, a moment later, Brant was able to observe the corpse of the predator, slain probably by the laser rifle the younger of the two strangers was holding. The sandcat was bigger than a Bengal tiger, and curiously catlike in appearance, for all that it was reptilian.

The two men he observed narrowly as he rode up to where they stood. One was a native, lean and wolfish, holding a bright new laser rifle at high port, not exactly pointing the weapon at the mounted man, but having it ready for action at need. He had hard, cold eyes and a cruel, thin-lipped mouth, and Brant noticed that his garment bore no clan markings, which suggested that he was *aoudh*—an outlaw, exiled from his nation.

The other man, rather surprisingly, was an Earthsider, older than Brant by a couple of decades, probably, wearing a fresh nioflex suit but without a respirator, which meant his body chemistry and lungs had been surgically modified to endure Martian conditions. Brant himself had undergone these modifications years before, and knew that few colonists save for the Colonial Administration police can afford to have their bodies adjusted to life in the open on the desert world.

However, the older man did not look like a cop to Brant, and he would have been extremely surprised to have discovered that the police were looking for him this far from Sun Lake City. Nevertheless, Brant had not kept alive this long on Mars without learning how to take precautions.

He reined in the loper a little distance from where the two men and the dead beasts were stationed, and slid down from the saddle. He held one of his power guns in his left hand, the barrel pointing down, but ready for use if necessary.

The older man stepped forward, raising one hand in salute.

"Good day, citizen! I am Dr. Will Harbin, an Aresologist, and this is my guide, Agila. We are fortunate that you came along."

"Jim Brant," said the newcomer, with a curt nod to the native guide. "Prospecting. These two women are under my protection," he added, as the two plodded up to where the loper stood.

He looked the scene over, noticing a second loper, seemingly unharmed, which knelt exhaustedly on the sand.

"Looks like you had a run-in with a sandcat," he observed. "Lucky it didn't get all of your beasts."

Will Harbin smiled wearily. "That we did, Cn. Brant. My man, Agila, brought it down just as it went after our pack-beast."

Brant was a trifle puzzled. "Why are you just sitting here, instead of piling everything on the lopers? The cliffwall isn't very far away—"

Harbin shrugged. "We've been riding across the dustland for days now, trying to make for the Regio before our mounts foundered. The beasts are too exhausted to travel farther, and we sure weren't looking forward to spending another night out here—not with the chance of more sandcats on the prowl!"

"Right," grunted Brant. "The scent of the slain beasts will bring them around by nightfall. Better chance it afoot and lead your beasts at any easy pace. We'll accompany you, of course. No sandcat is going to be crazy enough to risk attacking three men and two women. The quicker we get started, the better.''

Harbin followed Brant's advice, and, while Agila and the women loaded the saddlebags on the weary beast, the two Earthsiders drew aside for a brief conversation.

"Are you looking for anything in particular on the Regio, or just making a survey?'' inquired Brant.

Will Harbin smiled: "Actually, I'm fossil-hunting, Martian paleontology being one of my fields. But as far as the Administration knows, I'm making a photo-survey of this part of the south.'' He grinned. "What they don't know, won't hurt them, I figure!''

Brant chuckled. "Money's scarce for fossil-hunting, I guess?'' The older man soberly agreed.

"Mind telling me where you picked up this guide of yours?''

"In Dakhshan, the trade city,'' he said. Brant nodded. Few and very far between were the permanent settlements of the People, but Dakhshan was the nearest—a sheltered spot where many merchant routes met.

"What do you know about him? Looks *aoudh*, to me. . . .''

"Yes, Agila was driven into exile by a powerful native chieftain who envied him his prowess and his wealth,'' said Harbin. "Or so *he* says, anyway.''

Brant said nothing, chewing it over. Most outlaws profess innocence of any wrongdoing as a matter of course, whether they were actually innocent or not. He didn't much like the looks of this Agila: the man had the hard, wolfish way of a bandit, to his observance.

All bandits are outlaws, of course. So . . . if he was right about this Agila, what possible crime could he have committed that was deemed so horrendous that even the bandits would force him into flight?

It was an interesting question.

And, as it had weight to bear on their immediate future, he decided to find the answer to it as soon as possible.

II

THE PURSUIT

6

The Night

On their way back to the cliffwall, the two Earthsiders conversed further, getting to know each other. Brant was convinced that Will Harbin was no police marshal, hence he had given the older man his proper name. Marshals run to a younger breed, harder in the face, shrewder about the eyes.

Harbin cleared his throat at one point. "Ah, these women of yours . . . are they your—wives?"

Brant had to laugh. Then he explained how he had stumbled upon them, staked out to die in the ruined city on the plateau. Harbin nodded thoughtfully.

"That must have been Ythiom," he murmured, "the best preserved of the ancient ruins atop the Ogygis Regio. I'd hoped to visit it on my return journey, for I'm planning to end up in Sun Lake City."

They talked further, and, as they talked, Agila plodded along in the rear of the party, leading the pack-loper. More rested from its ordeal by now, the beast was spruce enough to bear plump little Suoli. Nor was Agila at all displeased by this turn of events.

He had been rather long without enjoying a woman, had Agila, and to happen upon two of them, both young and both, in different ways, desirable, seemed to him a stroke of luck. Perhaps the Timeless Ones were smiling upon his fortunes at last, he thought to himself—that being the People's term for their mysterious gods.

The first woman, Zuarra, was too tall for his taste, and, with her close-cropped russet furcap, altogether too boyish.

But the second was a choice morsel, he thought to himself. He liked his women soft, plump, submissive.

Stealing a glance at her as she swayed listlessly in the saddle, clutching the saddle bow with both weak, ineffectual hands, he licked his thin cruel lips, dreaming of what might yet come of this chance meeting. . . .

When they reached the cliffwall, they unburdened the lopers and let the two women prepare the midday meal, for it was afternoon by now and they had long fasted and were hungry.

Squatting on his hams a few paces from the others, Agila studied the soft little woman narrowly, catching her startled gaze a time or two, on which occasion he gave her an admiring grin. Flustered, the girl blushed and looked hastily away; but, when she thought that the guide might not be observing, she stole a quick glance or two at him herself.

After the meal, Brant explained to the older man his intention of riding along the base of the cliffs until they discovered a large ravine in which to take shelter for the night. Harbin nodded, drew a microviewer from his gear, and flipped the dial for a brief time.

"There's just the sort of place you're looking for about two kilometers south of here," he remarked. "That is, if the CA Air Reconnaissance photomaps can be trusted. At even a moderate pace, we should be able to reach it well before nightfall—that is, if you have no objections to our joining you?"

Brant shook his head. "Not at all; glad of some companionship," he grunted. Always safety in number, he knew.

They mounted up and rode on, with Harbin mounted upon his own pack-loper and Zuarra taking her turn atop Brant's steed. As they rode, the scientist studied the exposed rock-strata and the loose gravel which carpeted the sands at the base of the cliffwall. His sharp eyes discerned many interesting fossils, uniformly of marine life, left over from the time, eons before, when this had been the bottom of a long-forgotten ocean.

He eyed them a bit wistfully, but said nothing. True, he

would very much have liked to take some samples, but in order to reach their destination and make camp before nightfall, they should keep moving. Besides, there would be many more fossils up ahead, he knew, and just as appetizing as these.

From time to time, Harbin studied the dials on the pack of instruments he wore slung about his chest, and made a small, neat notation on the pad he wore at his waist. The geographical relief map he would eventually create from these notes would comprise the most scrupulously detailed and accurate survey ever made of these uninhabited southern parts of the planet—the CA Survey maps having been put together in a photomontage of footage taken by one or another of the permanent satellite stations in close orbit about Mars.

The rest of the time, he studied Brant. He wondered who he truly was and what had brought him down to these inhospitable and desolate regions. He did not for one moment believe Brant to be a prospector as he had claimed to be: for one thing, he was completely ignorant of geology, as Harbin had shrewdly established during their earlier conversation with a few casual observations on the strata.

For another, he carried no geiger.

Well, he shrugged philosophically to himself, half the Earthsider denizens of Mars were exiled here for crimes or political offenses, or were at least the children of those earlier convict-settlers who had first established the domed Colonial cities. Brant could be anything from a gun-runner to a slaver, from a hunted thief or killer to a smuggler of archaeological treasures stolen from rifled tombs.

It didn't much matter to Harbin. He rather liked the big, grim man with the hard face, rather admired the strength and toughness of him.

Time would tell if they were to be friends. For the moment, at least they were not enemies. . . .

As the sun was descending into the west, they reached a place where the massive plateau was deeply cleft by a wide ravine that might have been the bed of a primordial river. This was the spot Will Harbin had suggested, and, looking it over, Brant felt satisfied. It would afford them a safe haven against the night, and the strata here were not as loose and crumbling as was the cliff they had descended when they had been attacked by the rock dragon.

It did not look to him as if they would have to worry about rock dragons here. While Agila and the two women unsaddled the lopers and set up the tents, Harbin and Brant combined their one-strand protective fences into one which was, by a narrow margin, just large enough to encompass the double-sized camp.

This was a natural precaution to take, although it was unlikely that any sandcats were to be found this close to the cliffs, as the great predators generally made their lairs and hunting grounds in the deep dustlands.

There were four tents to be erected, one for each of them, with the lopers tethered to pegs driven in the loose shale in the center of the encampment. This done, and the beasts set to munching on their plant-fiber cakes, the women lit liquid fire in the metal pan and prepared the evening meal.

There was still a few cutlets left over from the fat lizard that Brant had slain on the plateau, as well as the remnants of the canned goods and concentrates which Brant had brought with him from Sun Lake City. To these were now added the fresh supplies which Harbin had purchased in the native marts of Dakhshan much more recently.

All in all, they made a good meal and turned in for the night. With the electric fence switched on there was no real need to take turns at sentry-go, Brant knew.

Still and all, he felt restless and decided to take a turn or two about the perimeter of the camp before seeking his rest.

Others, as well, were not ready for sleep. From the tent wherein the two women had retired for the night, one came forth to stare at the starblaze. And from the inky shadows of another tent, Agila glided into the open, stopping short as he observed the woman come forth.

In the dim almost-dark of the Martian night, Agila could not at once be certain which of the two women had emerged from the tent to share the darkness with him. But he assumed it to be the soft, plump one whom he fancied.

Gliding on soundless steps to where she stood, staring up at the glory of the stars, the cowl of her robes concealing her features from him, he laid a cajoling arm about her shoulders and reached with the other hand for her breasts.

Startled, she turned in his embrace, and as she did so the hood of her robes fell back upon her shoulders, revealing the face of Zuarra.

Well, it was not the one he preferred, but it was all one to Agila. Grinning wolfishly, he insinuated one hand into the opening of her robes to capture a firm, pointed breast, while his other arm tightened about her so that she should not writhe free and his thin lips bent to seek her own in a hungry kiss—

A kiss that was never quite consummated.

A hand clamped his lean shoulder in a grip of iron; another closed about his throat, tearing him from the woman. Then a balled fist sank into his belly and he fell gagging to the sand, clutching for the long knife that slept in its dragonskin scabbard at his thigh, under his kilt.

But Brant kicked him in the face, knocking most of the fight out of the guide, who fell sprawling on his back and lay there gasping and spitting like a beached flounder.

Zuarra had fallen to her knees. Now Brant bent to help her to her feet, nor did she repulse his gesture.

For a moment, he held her against his chest as she clung to him, panting.

For a moment, her eyes, lustrous as wet dark jewels in the dim light, stared up into his own.

Then—

"This is the third time you have rescued me, O Brant," she whispered. "First, when my own people had staked me out to die, and you, a stranger and a *f'yagh*, cut my bonds and gave me to drink of your own water. Then, when I swooned under the stare of the rock dragon, and my own 'sister' forbore to come to my aid. And now, when this hungry dog of the Outlands would have laid his hands and his mouth upon me against my will. Why do you do these things, O Brant?"

"Because I am a man, and you are a woman," he said. To

his own ears, the words sounded absurd and foolish, savoring of outmoded chivalry. But he could think of nothing else to say.

She stared at him.

"Am I truly a woman, then, O Brant?" she asked.

"Woman enough for me or any other man," he said in thick tones.

She turned away without speaking and re-entered the tent she shared with the other woman. Brant looked around. While these few words had been exchanged, Agila had scuttled to the safety of his tent, avoiding further punishment.

Brant shrugged, and went to bed. But not to sleep. For the memory of huge eyes like lustrous, wet jewels haunted his restless thoughts almost till dawn. . . .

7

The Riders

After breakfast the next morning, Brant set Agila to digging a trench for their latrine.

He had briefly considered speaking to Will Harbin about the guide's behavior, but dismissed the notion. He felt certain that Agila had learned his lesson and would leave the women alone. Nor did he exchange words with the guide, merely asking him to hand over the dirk the fellow wore, which the other did grudgingly and with a sullen look in his eyes. The long knife Brant gave to Zuarra for her own protection.

Then they sat beneath the awnings and watched as Agila, grumbling and spitting Martian curses under his breath, toiled for three hours at digging the latrine trench.

Brant and Harbin made a circuit of the encampment, studying the dust-soft sands. There were no markings to be seen about the limits of the protective fence, which suggested to them that the camp had been in no danger of beasts during the night. This relieved them of one worry, but another was not long in arising. . . .

In midmorning, Will Harbin, aided by Zuarra, went prowling up the ravine, searching for maritime fossils. About the same time, Brant, with Agila, went hunting for game. They rode out into the dustlands, and, finding naught, searched farther along the edges of the cliff, and brought down two fat reptiles whose meat would serve to replenish their larder.

Suoli was left alone to tend to the feeding of the lopers and the cleansing of the cookpots and utensils. These menial tasks she performed without complaint, but who could know what resentments smoldered within the depths of her being?

The day passed slowly, as the travelers rested from the exertions of their long journey. Brant and Agila returned at length to the camp with fat reptiles and fodder for the riding beasts; toward sunfall, Doc Harbin and Zuarra came back to the encampment, the Earthsider scientist jubilant over the discovery of rare fossils of marine life, the woman with little interest in such things, and relieved to be able to rest, after an afternoon of clambering about the rock-strata in search of lumps of stone whose import was incomprehensible to her.

Brant and Agila, during the hunt, had exchanged few words and had seldom looked at each other. As Brant had imagined would be the case, the Martian guide was subdued, saying little, never referring to the events of the previous night, and for his part, Brant had been equally reticent. They both knew about hunting, and simply did the job.

The evening meal that night was shared in silence, each busy with his or her own thoughts. Brant noticed that between Zuarra and Suoli was little converse and less interchange of looks than before. It would seem evident that between the two "sisters" loomed the failure of Suoli to come to Zuarra's defense when the rock dragon had attacked.

Brant's lips twisted in a private, bitter smile, but he said nothing.

Will Harbin, however, waxed voluble, after the meal, jubilant over the discovery of so many important fossils. This ancient ocean, he said, had been one of the largest and most important on all of Mars, and had served to link many significant and wealthy maritime nations eons ago. Among the fossil remains he had uncovered that afternoon were at least four previously unrecorded by Earthsider scientists.

Brant was not particularly impressed, and said little by way of comment. The rest of the meal was passed without further speech.

Once the beasts were seen to and the protective fence energized, the members of the party sought their rest.

Brant was just dozing off when he was roused to alertness

by the catlike scratching of long nails at the sealed flap of his tent. He spoke in inquiry, and the answer roused him in every sense of the word.

"It is Zuarra, O Brant—"

Loins tingling and blood surging high, the Earthsider sprang to his feet and covered his nakedness with a loose robe. He unseamed the tent and Zuarra slipped within.

Pulses drumming, Brant caught her in his arms, but she disengaged herself with agility.

"I am not come here for *that* purpose, Brant," she said. Her voice was breathless and urgent, not seething with contempt, so he took no particular offense.

"What is it, then?" he demanded.

"Come outside," she breathed.

He secured his garments, and buckled on the gun-belt, and followed her outside the tent. The starblaze lit the skies of Mars in scintillant glory, as ever, but the luminance thereof was dim, being moonless. He stared about.

"What is it, woman?"

She pointed wordlessly toward the ridgeline of the antique continent above where they camped.

"A watcher on the heights," she whispered. "He has been there for the better part of an hour."

Brant looked and saw the mounted man looming in dark silhouette against the glitter of a thousand stars. His jaw tightened and his face went grim.

"Who can it be?" he muttered under his breath, but the Martian woman heard his words.

"Someone who scouts for a greater number," she said tersely. "But I know not for what purpose."

"Bandits? Raiders? Outlaws?"

She shrugged. "Mayhap, O Brant."

He thought to himself: *Or slavers.*

But it didn't make sense to him, not completely. Slavers or bandits would have no particular reason to risk their guns for so small a party of travelers.

"Shall we wake the others?" Zuarra asked in low tones.

Brant shrugged. "I suppose so," he said gruffly.

*   *   *

Beside Brant's brace of power guns and Zuarra's long knife, they had only Will Harbin's twin laser rifles wherewith to defend themselves against attack by the natives.

There were now two riders on the ridge above them.

"Who do you think they are, Jim?" asked Harbin. Brant said nothing, merely shrugged. There was no way to hazard a guess as to the identity of the riders. They could be anybody.

The thing was, there were no native clans encamped in these parts so near the southern pole.

The older man inquired of Agila his opinion. But the guide only made the Martian gesture that was equivalent to a shrug, voicing no opinion. He looked nervous and tense to Brant's eyes, but the big man said nothing.

Suoli squeaked and fluttered nervously. Brant asked of Zuarra if she thought the riders were scouts of her people. He knew that if the Moon Hawk nation had discovered that the two women staked out to die had been set free by the hand of a *f'yagh* they might resent the interference enough to come after them. But somehow he doubted it. As did Zuarra.

"At this season, they are encamped to the north," she said tonelessly, "in regions about Khorahd. Nor are such as Zuarra and Suoli important enough to merit pursuit, O Brant."

Brant had thought as much, himself. Still and all, it did no harm to ask.

By moonrise the two riders had left the high ridge and were nowhere to be seen. Nor was there any further sign of them that night, although Harbin, Agila and Brant stood guard, each in turn, while the women slept.

With dawn, the travelers held a brief council, trying to decide what to do for their own protection. Brant pointed out that now that their camp had been discovered, they were exposed to danger. It would seem that the scouts had ridden back to join a larger force, but whether or not this force was interested in pursuing and attacking them was an unanswerable question.

No one had any better idea to present, so for the moment they decided to remain in their present camp, simply standing guard day and night against the chance of attack.

Neither that day nor all that next night, nor the following day did the unknown riders show themselves again. The travelers began to relax, seeming to have little enough to fear.

"Perhaps they were but travelers such as we," suggested Zuarra over a frugal meal, "alert and wary in these untraveled regions, but uninterested in attacking us."

Brant shrugged, saying nothing. But it was true than bandits or raiders would normally have little interest in so small a party as were they. And few native clans would risk the Earthsider power guns with so little to gain. After all, there were only three men, two women and three beasts. . . .

"Maybe it would be better to break camp under cover of darkness and move farther south," suggested Doc Harbin. Brant thought about it briefly.

"Maybe, Doc," he grunted. "But we have a secure position here, with our back to the steep cliffs. They can hardly come at us down the cliffs, for their beasts would find them hard to negotiate, and we could fire from below while their hands were busy guiding the beasts down. On the other hand, if they came after us while we were on the run, they would have *us* at a disadvantage."

The older man nodded thoughtfully. "And, for that matter, why should they come at us at all, since we have done them no harm?" he said.

Brant agreed.

But he noticed the guilty flush that darkened the sullen features of Harbin's guide.

For some reason, the man seemed afraid, did Agila.

But . . . *why?*

8

Watching Eyes

When they rose with dawn and left their tents to scan the ridgeline far above, it was empty. Whoever it had been that had spied upon their camp the night before had evidently moved on. Perhaps they had been mere travelers, after all.

But somehow Brant doubted it. Pessimist that he was, he had always found that when you anticipate the worst you are seldom surprised. But he said nothing of this to the others.

They busied themselves with the morning tasks, tending to the lopers, preparing a meal. And they were an oddly uncommunicative group, Brant had to notice. Agila performed his duties in a sullen manner, avoiding all eyes; Zuarra seemed lost in her own thoughts, while little Suoli kept timidly to herself and stayed out of her "sister's" way as much as possible.

Even Harbin had little enough to say. He became lost in the pleasant occupation of fossil-hunting in the loose shale which lay heaped at the foot of the crumbling cliffs, and that afternoon he kept to his tent, sorting and classifying his finds.

Taking the lopers, Brant and Agila went hunting. It took them an hour and a little more to find a rock lizard, which they slew and skinned before returning to their encampment. While they were doing this, Brent scanned the ridgeline—it had become a habit, almost automatic, to do this by now.

And he saw four watchers. They were trying not to be seen, crouched low on the ridge, dark hooded robes blending with the harsh stone. Perhaps he would not have seen them at all had not the sunlight momentarily reflected from a glass lens.

The watchers were using binoculars. . . .

All the rest of that day Brant felt the nape-hairs on his neck prickle under the scrutiny of those watching eyes far above. If the unknown watchers were raiders, outlaws, enemies of whatever nature, from the vantage of their height they could pick the members of the encampment off one by one with a laser rifle.

If they were armed with energy weapons, that is. Which they undoubtedly were. Brant's thin lips twisted in a slight, sour and cynical grin: Colonial Administration law made it the highest of crime to sell guns to the natives, but the law was difficult, nearly impossible, to enforce. And Brant had run guns to more than a few of the native princelings in his time.

It would be a bitter irony if one of those guns were to slay him now, he thought with grim humor.

The women had prepared the evening meal earlier than usual. After they were through eating and had tended to the beasts, Brant sought out Harbin for a conference. He found the scientist still hunched over his fossils, examining them through a lens and from time to time making a brief entry in the small black notebook he carried.

"Doc, you got a minute?" he asked.

"Certainly. As a matter of fact, I could use a break," the older man remarked, rubbing his eyes tiredly. He gave Brant a shrewd glance. "What's up?"

Brant shrugged. "Small council of war," he said. Then, as the older man listened without comment, Brant told him about the watchers on the height.

"Four of them now," grunted Harbin, rubbing his lean jaw. "Who do you suppose they are, Jim?"

"No idea," Brant admitted. "But they're up to no good, that's for sure. Ordinary travelers wouldn't have hung around ever since last night, just to keep an eye on us. . . ."

"Well, they could hardly be the authorities, because we're doing nothing illegal," mused Harbin reflectively. "And, besides, I've never heard of the police riding the Highlands—don't they usually use aircraft?''

Brant nodded.

"So . . . they must be natives. But what could they possibly want from us? They must have their own lopers, so they shouldn't be all that interested in stealing ours . . . true, the tents and weapons are of value, but—d'you suppose they could have seen the women? In those voluminous robes, a woman doesn't look much different from a man. . . ."

"You're thinking they might be slavers?" Brant said slowly. Of course, the same possibility had occurred to him. The older man nodded, then shrugged.

"Anything's possible, here in the Drylands," he remarked. "And they have to be after something!"

Brant shook his head slowly.

"It's hard to believe even slavers would risk a fight with three armed men, just for a couple of women. Especially since they can't have gotten a clear enough look at either of them to know whether they're young and attractive. After all, for all they know Zuarra and Suoli might be a couple of old crones we fetched along just to do the cooking."

Harbin chuckled quietly at that. Then, sobering:

"Well, Jim, what do you think we ought to do about our nosey friends on the ridgeline?"

Brant had been considering that problem all day. "We've got three possible courses of action," he said. "In the first place, we could simply sit here pretending we don't know they're there, while keeping on the alert, of course. That way we force them to make the first move . . . or give up and ride away."

"But that means giving the initiative to our unknown friends," Doc pointed out. "And if they mean to attack us, why should we give them the advantage of picking the best time—and ground?"

Brant nodded in agreement. "Right; so the second course would be to climb the ridge and confront them—taking them by surprise, since I don't think they realize that we know they're up there."

"But they would see us climbing, and if they mean to pick

a fight—for whatever reason—they could hardly wish for a more perfect opportunity. It's hard to fight back when you're hanging on to the wall of a cliff.''

''Yeah, there's no question about that,'' growled the younger man. ''So . . . only thing left to do is sneak out under cover of darkness and put as much distance between us and them as we can, before they find out next morning that we have skedaddled.''

''So what's your plan?'' inquired Harbin.

''We make 'em think we're all bedded down for the night. Leave the tents up and some light going. Then we take the bedding, the supplies, mount up and ride out.''

''The nights get damned cold in these parts,'' the scientist observed. ''And they'll seem a lot colder without the insulation of the tents.''

''I know, but they'll have somebody keeping an eye on us, and if they see us striking the tents and packing our gear, that'll be a dead giveaway. If they're planning to pick a fight, they'll have to do it then and there, before we put too much distance between us.''

He paused, rubbing his jowls.

''On the other hand,'' he mused thoughtfully, ''that might not be a bad idea. It'll be to their disadvantage to fight us in the dark, because it would be next to impossible to climb down the cliffs by night. And if they fire on us, we can aim at the flare of their guns. There's plenty of fallen rocks and boulders around here for us to use as shields against their weapons, and we can keep moving from spot to spot between shots, so they'll have a hellova problem figuring out where we are at any given time.''

Harbin thought it over, and agreed it looked like the best course of action open to them.

''They won't dare try to get their lopers down the cliffs in the dark, so don't you think it likely—unless they decide to fire on us after all—that once they know we're moving out, they'll ride along the ridgeline, hoping to keep up with us?''

Brant grinned. ''They'll have a hard time figuring which direction we're going, north or south. So they'll have to split up, two of 'em going one way, the rest in the other direction.

If nothing else, it'll cut their numbers in half and double our chances of winning, if it comes to a fight!''

They talked the plan over, looking for loopholes that hadn't yet occurred to them.

They found none. It would be touch and go, but the only alternatives to taking that risk looked even riskier.

"So when you suggest we make our move?" inquired Harbin.

Brant grinned wolfishly.

"Right now," he growled.

9
The Flight

While the older scientist went to order Agila to pack their gear as unobtrusively as possible, Brant sauntered casually over to the other tents to inform the women of this decision.

Zuarra listened without comment, and nodded grim agreement. She did not question the urgency of the problem, neither did she bother to remark on the risk and danger involved in flight.

Suoli, of course, was timid and reluctant, and needed more reassurance than Brant felt inclined to give.

"Listen," he said roughly, "I can't make any guarantees! Sure, we're taking a big chance, but we're already in trouble and this looks like the best, maybe the only, way out."

"But to leave the tents!" the little woman wailed, wringing her soft plump hands. "In the night we will freeze—!"

"So we bundle together for warmth, or look for a cave where we can set up one of the heaters. We don't have much choice in the matter, don't you understand?"

Zuarra spoke up. "Is it that you intend abandoning your *f'yagha* energy barrier, when we ride out?" she asked. Brant nodded somberly.

"Too much of a problem dismantling it," he pointed out. "Too much chance of them seeing us at it, and realizing what we're going to do."

"Then wherever we make camp, we will be in danger of beasts," said Zuarra.

Brant shrugged impatiently.

"So we'll take turns standing guard!" he growled. "C'mon,

53

we're wasting time—pack your stuff. Since we're all going to
have to ride, we can't load down the lopers. Bring bedding,
all the food, and the pressure-still. Leave everything else."

With those curt words, he strode out of the tent to pack his
own gear.

Thirty minutes later they were riding across the sands.

The lopers hadn't had much work to do recently, and were
fresh and well-rested. Doubling up in the saddle was
uncomfortable, but there was no alternative. If one or another
of them had to travel on foot, the pace of their flight would
be slowed.

Suoli cast a wistful backward glance at the dim lights in
the warm tents, and began sobbing breathlessly to herself.
Save for her muffled weeping, they rode in silence.

It was Brant's plan to strike out at angles from the cliffwall,
and ride some considerable distance into the dustlands. This
would make it exceedingly difficult for the watchers on the
ridge to spot them, for the moaning winds of Mars had carved
the fine, dustlike powder into rolling dunes taller than a grown
man.

When they had gone far enough to his liking, they angled
directly south and followed the curving line of the now-
distant cliffs.

As far as they could tell, the unknown watchers had not
discovered their quarry to be in flight. Probably (grinned
Brant sourly to himself) they were huddled in uncomfortable
slumber on the cold rock far above, envying those in the
encampment below, whom they assumed sleeping cozily in
the insulated tents.

Well, come morning, they were in for a surprise.

Brant was almost sorry that the watchers had not discovered their plan and begun firing, for it would be a vast relief
to know just what the watchers intended. However, the ink-
black darkness had concealed their furtive departure from the
watchful eyes above and it did not seem likely that their
absence would be discovered before morning.

There was one problem which bothered him and made him

a trifle uneasy. And that was, quite simply, that in order to leave the encampment they had been forced to switch off the power fence. There was no alternative to this, for the lopers would have suffered from the energy-laden wires when they rode over them as much as would beasts of prey, for whom the energy fence was designed. But if a predator should choose to enter the camp during the night, to rip open the tents in search of food, surely the rumpus would attract the attention of the watchers, and their flight would be known.

Brant shrugged the problem aside. "The hell with it," he grumbled to himself. "You can't take every damn precaution—and maybe our luck will hold."

By this time they had put several miles between them and the abandoned camp, and the lopers were weary of laboring through the talcum-fine dust. So Brant headed in to the shelter of the cliffs, where rock outcroppings and pulverized shale would give the beasts easier footing, and enable them to make better time.

It was his intention to ride all night long, and then, when morning came, to hole up somewhere, seeking shelter in the side of the cliffs, where caves and crevices could easily be found. He just hoped that these wouldn't already be affording shelter to rock dragons or something even bigger, more powerful and more dangerous. But, as he'd just decided, you have to take *some* risks.

Zuarra was sharing the saddle with him, as she disdained to ride with Agila. For all the danger of their precipitous night ride, and all the various hazards and problems he had on his mind, Brant could not help feeling uncomfortably aware of the proximity of her body to his.

Her hair held a faint trace of perfume—bitter, musky, a dry, spicelike scent that reminded him vaguely of cinnamon.

Her arms were tightly wound about his waist, for she was riding behind him so that he could more easily handle the reins. So close was her embrace, that even through his clothing he could feel the soft pressure of her firm breasts nuzzling into his back.

He tried not to notice that her smooth thigh was pressed against his leg, and that her warm breath panted against his nape. But Brant was only a man, not a priest or a saint, and the warm closeness of their bodies aroused hungers within him, as did the delicious fragrance of her hair.

Muttering an uncomfortable curse, he moved his big shoulders restively, trying to turn his attention to other matters.

It is doubtful whether Zuarra could have understood his words, for they were in English. But women possess certain instincts, and in the windy dark she smiled a slow little smile to herself, understanding the cause of his irritable agitation.

The night seemed endless, and as they swayed in the saddle to the rhythm of the beast's awkward gait, they found themselves being lulled into sleep. Brant almost fell from the saddle at one point, but Zuarra's grasp restrained him, and he straightened, stiffening his back, forcing sleepiness from his mind by an act of will.

The lopers themselves were beginning to founder by this time, for the beasts were unaccustomed to being driven for so long at their best pace. Eventually, and with reluctance, Brant had to give the signal to slow down and let the beasts canter at an easier pace, to conserve their vigor.

Dawn took them all by surprise. On this harsh desert world, where the air is incredibly thin, sunrise does not advertise its coming by the slow brightening of light, as it does on Earth, with its thicker, more humid atmosphere. No, dawn is like a vast, silent explosion, which comes upon you with no advance warnings.

One moment they were riding through pitch-black gloom. And, in the next instant of time, daylight flooded the sky and they blinked sleepy eyes against the unexpected brilliance.

Brant pulled up and let Zuarra dismount. Then he got down from the saddle himself, stretching weary legs with a jaw-cracking yawn.

"We'll take a brief rest stop here," he advised the others. After a long night spent in the saddle, they were all thankful for an opportunity to relieve their bladders.

Brant and Harbin scanned the ridgeline narrowly, through powerful binoculars, but nowhere could they discern the slightest sign of the unknown watchers. That was one problem off Brant's mind, at least.

"How far do you think we traveled, Doc?" inquired Brant, wetting his lips with a drink from his canteen. The scientist pursed his lips and hazarded a guess.

Brant grunted. "Better than I could have hoped," he said. "Well, we're all worn out, and the lopers are in bad shape. What say we find a place to hole up and get some shut-eye?"

"I could use some," admitted Harbin with a rueful grin. "Not as young as I used to be. . . ."

Brant chuckled at that. "You're made out of whipcord and steel wire, and you know it," he quipped. "Matter of fact, you look like you're in better shape than I am."

This part of the shoreline of the prehistoric continent was grooved and worn into deep gullies, and it didn't take the travelers very long to find a snug cave. Fortunately, although the crusted droppings suggested it had once served as a rock dragon's lair, the beast was no longer in residence, and had not been for many years.

The women unrolled the bedding and Harbin asked the younger man as to the wisdom of mounting guard.

Brant stifled another huge yawn, and shook his head blearily.

"Naw, I don't think so. They're just now realizing we skipped out last night, and have no way of knowing which way we rode, or how far we went. It'll be quite a while before they catch up to us, that is, if they bother with pursuit. And that shale we were riding over most of the night won't show tracks."

They went to bed and almost instantly fell asleep.

10

The Riddle

Bone-weary as they all were, it was well into the afternoon before any of them awoke.

Brant stretched tired muscles and yawned a jaw-cracking yawn. Then he got up and went out of the narrow cave to relieve himself. He found Harbin already up and dressed.

"I figured you'd still be snoozing," the big Earthsider grunted. The older man smiled ruefully.

"Old bones don't rest easy," Harbin admitted. "People of my age don't need that much sleep, you know. After all, the Big Sleep is nearer for us than for you young folks."

Brant grimaced and spat. "Hell, Doc, you'll see me in my grave, more than likely. Anybody else up?"

Will Harbin shook his head briefly. Stepping away from the cliffwall, Brant scanned the ridgeline with slow and careful gaze.

"Any signs of company?" he inquired.

Harbin shook his head again. "None that I can discern," he said. "But I hardly suppose that they will be on our track this quickly."

"Let's hope not, anyway," Brant growled. "Another ride like the one we had last night will about do me in!"

Agila emerged from the mouth of the cave shortly thereafter. He ignored Brant as best he might, greeting his employer briefly. Before long, the delicious smell of food being cooked was on the air. Brant sniffed hungrily.

"Soup's on, I guess. That means the women must be up."

They broke their fast ravenously, and seldom had hot food tasted better to any of the travelers.

Later on, having fed the lopers, Brant saddled his beast and rode out into the midst of the dunes. Climbing to the top of the tallest one he could find easily, he spent a long time carefully searching the ridgeline with his binoculars. Eventually, finding no slightest sign of their pursuers, he remounted his steed and rode back to the cave, reporting his discovery, or lack of any discovery, to the old scientist.

"Thing is, do we hole up here or keep goin'?" Brant concluded.

"I thought you were the leader of this miniature expedition," Harbin remarked lightly.

The other shrugged. "Doesn't matter who's boss. You've got the brains and all the know-how; I got the muscle and the wilderness experience. So what d'you think? Stay, or keep movin'?"

Harbin chewed it over thoughtfully. Finally, he said:

"Our friends will have to split into two groups, one riding north and the other heading south, since they have no way of knowing in which direction we went. Just as you surmised yesterday. And, that is, if they *are* still tracking us."

"So?"

"So, even if they come this way, and are still riding the high country, they'll have no chance of seeing us, providing that we keep to the cave."

Brant shook his head. "Wrong, Doc. What if they have a pack of hunters?"

Hunters were small, fleet domesticated reptiles used by the Martian natives for much the same purpose as Earthsiders use hunting dogs. They possessed a remarkable sense of smell, and could easily have detected the odors of cooking food or fresh droppings from the lopers, even from the ridgeline.

Harbin scratched his nose. "I didn't see any hunters before," he said. Brant shrugged.

"Neither did I. But that doesn't mean they don't have 'em. If I gotta gamble my life, I'd like it to be on a sure thing."

"So you think we should keep moving, eh?"

Brant looked stubborn. "Goes against my grain to run from a fight," he admitted heavily. "But they outnumber us and probably are better armed. We got a good head start on them right now, and it might be smart to hang onto that advantage."

"We simply can't keep running forever," Harbin observed shrewdly, "and I, for one, would like to be sure they are still after us, before I continue this flight from a trouble that may, after all, no longer be there."

"Not bad thinking, I guess," nodded Brant. "Besides, the lopers are still tired from that all-night ride. Let's hang around here for a while more, keeping a sentinel posted out on the dunes. We can take shifts. And there's something else . . . ?"

"Which is?" prompted the scientist.

Brant looked at him squarely.

"I want to find out *why* they're after us, whoever the hell they are. Any ideas?"

"None," said Harbin. Brant continued looking at him.

"Let's be square, Doc," he suggested. "I got some cops on my tail 'cause of a fight in a barroom back in Sun Lake City. I know it isn't cops we saw watching us from the high country. But outside of that, I'm clean. Oh, sure, you can't live a life like mine without making enemies, any more than you can make an omelet without cracking eggs. But there's just nobody that wants me bad enough to chase me into this part of the world. How about you?"

Harbin told him frankly that he was open and above board, and the sincerity in his voice was enough to convince Brant.

"But what about the two women?" the scientist asked. Brant made a negative gesture. Then he told Harbin how he had encountered the two staked out to die, and had rescued them. He concluded:

"Being outlawed and left to either die or fend for themselves on their own is punishment enough for their nation," he said. "I know the People well enough to know that."

"So do I," said the scientist. "That only leaves. . . ."

"Agila," growled Brant. "How much d'you know about him, anyway?"

"Not very much," Harbin admitted. "Only what he told me, which was cursory. He's an outcast, too, like the two women, but it might be that he is not exactly as innocent of wrongdoing as he wanted me to think at the time."

"Let's both keep our eyes on him, then," suggested Brant. They agreed.

Later that evening, Brant went out among the dunes to relieve Zuarra from sentry duty.

"Have you sighted anything?" he asked. "On the ridgeline or anywhere else?"

"Nothing, O Brant," she replied.

"Good!" he grunted. Then he mentioned briefly the matters he and the older man had discussed concerning Agila. And he asked her if she had noticed anything at all peculiar or out of the ordinary in the man's behavior."

"*That* one!" the woman sniffed contemptuously. "Zuarra has as little to do with the lean wolf as she may manage."

"You've never talked, then?" he inquired.

"As little as possible—since that night when he would lay unwanted hands upon Zuarra, and Brant felled him with a blow of his fist. Besides," she added stiffly, "that one now spends as much time as he can find in whispered converse with Suoli."

Brant suppressed a smile. All women are given to jealousy, he thought cynically to himself. Even those that eschew the embrace of men and choose their own sex for solace.

He began the slow, laborious climbing of the dune to its crest, wherefrom a clearer view of the surrounding country could be had. But before returning to their encampment, Zuarra turned to speak to him again. A sudden thought had struck her.

"Yes?" he inquired.

"It may perchance mean nothing at all, O Brant," the woman said hesitantly. "But Zuarra has noticed, of nights, before he seeks his pallet, the lean wolf removes something from his baggage, and sleeps with it cradled against his breast. It may very well have naught to do with our present predicament, but Zuarra wonders if Brant has noticed this puzzling act of Agila.''

He shook his head. "No, I haven't. And it may, after all, mean nothing, as you suggest. Or it may be the answer to the mystery of why the unknown strangers are on our trail . . . of what shape is the thing you speak of?''

She shrugged. "Circular and flat, but I have never caught a good look at it, for the wolf keeps it wrapped in oiled silks, and hidden in his baggage during the day. I but idly noticed it in passing, that is all.''

The woman nodded contentedly, and mounted and rode off in the direction of the camp, leaving the Earthsider alone with his own thoughts.

There had to be an answer to this puzzle, and Brant was determined to find it out, whatever the risk or the cost.

III

THE DESCENT

11
The Dish

The long hours of Brant's watch passed slowly, but without event. In time, timid little Suoli came riding out to take her turn as sentinel. He gruffly informed her that he had seen nothing at all worthy of note, and sternly warned her against falling asleep on duty. After all, the lives of them all might depend upon her alertness and vigilance.

Returning to camp, he turned in and caught a couple of hours of badly needed sleep. But he had determined to rouse at the time it was Agila's turn to be awakened for guard-duty, for he meant to have it out with the fellow before the night was done. While Agila was certainly entitled to his own privacy, and to the secrets of his heart, that privilege must yield when it might involve the lives and safety of all the others.

Brant had lived long enough in the wilderness of Mars to have developed that "inner clock" by which a man may wake himself at any particular time. The mental mechanism did not always work that well, depending, as it did, upon the extent of his exertions and the degree of his fatigue, but he relied upon it now to awaken him when it was time for Agila to get up in order to relieve Suoli.

This done, Brant fell at once into a deep, dreamless sleep from which he awoke a couple of hours later, refreshed and alert. The air was bitterly cold, the stars a blaze of diamond fire across the velvet heavens. Both moons were aloft at this period, but neither was at all visible, due to their extremely low albedo.

Brant rose and looked about him warily, closing the pressure-seams on his insulated suit. His inner mechanism had awakened him exactly at the right time, for a light was on in the small tent where Agila and the older scientist slept, and by its dim luminance, Brant saw the lean silhouette of the native guide as he donned his own garments. The big Earthsider strode on swift and silent feet to the double tent and opened the flap.

Agila shot him a swift, sharp, nervous glance. Harbin, roused by the lighting of the lamp, blinked curiously as Brant entered the tent and strode abruptly to the guide's bedroll. Agila uttered a short cry and his hand darted toward the blankets. But Brant's left hand closed upon his wrist with crushing force that wrung a squawk of pain from the other.

With his right hand, Brant dipped into the blankets and found a flat, hard, circular object closely wrapped in oiled silks. It was even as the Martian woman had informed him.

"What is this thing that you hide against your bosom when you sleep?" Brant demanded of Agila.

Hot resentment flared in the amber eyes of the native guide, but then he swiftly mastered the emotion, and presented a bland, smooth gaze free of emotion.

"It is a private matter and nothing that need concern the *f'yagha*," he muttered in sullen tones, dropping his gaze to Brant's boots.

"Everything is of concern to me, because I am the leader of this group of chance-met strangers—and I need to know why those people are pursuing us," growled Brant. Then he carefully began to unwrap the silk covering from the flat object.

Agila whined a curse, and one hand dipped to the knife scabbarded in his boot after the native custom. But Brant had expected that, and his power gun appeared almost miraculously in one capable fist. The cold stubby barrel of the weapon was aimed directly at the heart of Agila. Its cold black eye stared at him. Agila licked thin lips with a pointed tongue.

"Don't try it," Brant advised.

"My boy, would you mind awfully if I asked what all of this is about?" inquired Harbin querulously.

As he removed the wrappings from the discoid thing, Brant made his explanation in brusque terms.

"I see," mused the scientist. "Well, let's see what we've got here—"

Brant unwrapped a circular object of pale metal, slightly concave, like a ceremonial dish. The pallid gleam of the metal made his eyes narrow: it was "Martian gold," and the metal was rare and precious. There was writing on it of some sort, and a curious design of curving, meandering lines—both of which were meaningless to him.

With an expression of inquiry, Brant handed the gold dish to the older man, who examined it curiously, turning it from side to side so that the markings upon it could be seen in the dim light of the lamp.

"Well, Doc?"

Harbin cleared his throat uncertainly. "Old work; very old," he said tentatively. "Dozens of centuries, at least. Perhaps, dozens of millennia. No . . . millions of years, surely! See how the writing is worn almost to the point of illegibility? And the styling of the characters . . . that ancient variant of the written tongue was already very old when the oceans died."

"But what does the writing mean?" demanded Brant harshly, still covering Agila with his gun.

The older man shrugged helplessly.

"I haven't the faintest idea! Not my period at all. I am a specialist in Late Imperial and Early Dynasty Princedoms. Very little of this writing has ever been found, and even less has been translated. Even then, the translations were purely conjectural—informed guesswork, little more."

"Well . . . is the thing valuable?"

"Beyond any question, *very* valuable. The sort of treasure that might well become the precious racial heirloom of a clan chieftain, even a prince," said Harbin flatly.

They both looked at Agila. The guide cringed, licked dry lips again, then straightened to face them defiantly.

"The dish is mine!" he stated.

"Sure, if stolen property can be said to belong to the thief," grinned Brant. The native flinched.

He dropped his eyes again. "Mine," he repeated, but there was no conviction in his voice.

The two Earthsiders exchanged a glance.

"Old and valuable enough to be the treasured heirloom of a clan chieftain, eh?" muttered Brant grimly. "Which would explain why he's come hunting for the man that took it!"

Doc nodded slowly. "Now we know," he whispered. "At least, it's the easiest, and the most logical, explanation."

"Maybe we can beg a parley, and offer to return it," suggested Brant. "Along with the thief himself, of course."

"No! Masters! He will kill me—slowly!" cried Agila, his swarthy features whitening with fear.

The two Earthsiders grinned at each other.

"That's what I think the legal eagles would call an unforced admission of guilt," observed Will Harbin.

"All right, man, start talking," growled Brant. "Exactly who does the gold dish belong to? I mean, who is the man you stole it from?"

The defiance and bravado had drained out of Agila. His head was lowered and he rubbed his wrists with trembling fingers, for the strength of Brant's grip had bruised his flesh.

"His name is Tuan," muttered the thief. "Once he was a great hereditary chieftain, high in the councils of the Prince of the Moon Dragon Nation. He was defeated in war against a rival chieftain and his people were decimated. Long since, he became a homeless fugitive, an outlaw, with only a small band of warriors to follow him. . . ."

"But still retaining a lot of pride," guessed Brant. "And this heirloom is the only one of his hereditary treasures he held onto, right?"

"It is even as you say, *f'yagh*," Agila said in low tones.

At that point, Will Harbin spoke up.

"Jim . . . I've got a feeling that it wouldn't be enough to salve Tuan's injured pride, just to return the dish to him and to hand Agila over to his crude justice."

"Why not? What else could he want?"

"You forget that we're the hated *f'yagha*—the greedy Outworlders who have invaded and robbed and despoiled this world. And Tuan will know, or guess—or force Agila to admit—that we have seen and handled the heirloom. Profaned it with our eyes, with our touch, as he would probably put it."

"So . . . it's fight or run, then, eh? Or be destroyed," growled Brant.

"I'm afraid so," admitted Will Harbin. "Since we all pretty much agree that you're in command here, well—which is it to be? Fight, run, or die?"

"Run," said Brant briefly. And he nodded at the dish and at the thief. "But we leave these two—things—behind us when we do."

Agila squeaked and began to beg for mercy in a frenzied babbling voice, which both men ignored.

Doc stepped near. "Jim, what good will that do? I know the People, and as I've said, Tuan will be after us, no matter what we leave behind."

Brant grinned wolfishly, a hard baring of white teeth.

"Maybe," he grunted. "But dealing out his 'justice' to Agila will slow him up. Let's get packing!"

Even as they left the tent, bearing with them the precious golden dish and the knife which Agila had carried in his boot, a thin, far call came to their ears.

"Suoli!" exclaimed Brant. "She's on guard-duty right now—come on!"

Zuarra, having heard some commotion, emerged from her tent to look questioningly at Brant. Leaping into the saddle, he handed her one of his power guns, briefly instructing her to stand watch over Agila. Then he and Harbin, sharing the saddle, loped off in the direction from which the warning cry had sounded.

When they reached the dunes, Suoli came sliding down to point to the ridgeline.

"They are come, O Brant!" she wailed.

Brant studied the ridge through the binoculars. There were fourteen of them, by now.

He swore under his breath.

"Yes, and it looks like they have reinforcements."

12

The Discovery

They broke camp and made a run for it under cover of darkness. But Brant was getting awfully tired of running, and said so.

"Sooner or later, it's gotta come to a showdown between us—a fight," he growled, as they saddled the lopers. "And I'd wish it was sooner than later."

The older man said nothing, nodding silently. He knew that what truly irked Brant was the people under his care: two women, an old man, and a renegade. Brant would probably have taken a stand and fought it out, had it not been for them.

But fourteen warriors—for there were at least that many—were too many to fight with any real chance of victory. So . . . run they must, no matter how it irked the big Earthsider.

The one advantage in their favor was that, at least as yet, it would seem that none of the warriors of Tuan had been able to descend the cliffwall. This part of the shoreline of the prehistoric continent was too sheer to afford an easy descent, so all that Tuan and his war party could do was follow their route along the ridgeline.

Once Tuan got a sizable number of his followers down to their level, it would, of course, be a very different ballgame. But that time had not yet come.

As they rode out under cover of darkness, again abandoning some of their gear, Brant and Harbin conferred. Brant still felt that it would at least gain them time to leave the ancient golden dish behind, with the thief bound and helpless. Harbin again declined to agree with him, arguing that the insult to the clan-pride had been more than enough to rouse the ire of Tuan against the two of them, and the women, as well. Brant cursed under his breath, but in his heart he felt that the old scientist was probably right.

So they ran. But—to what haven?

Dawn broke, that sudden, silent explosion of pale light that illuminated the sky without warning, and they were still running. Mercifully, no riders were to be discovered on the ridgeline, which did not necessarily mean that they had outdistanced them, but just that the outlaw band was riding more cautiously than were they.

After a brief rest break and some food, they mounted up and rode on ever deeper into the south, seeking a safe haven. They doubled up in the saddle, for, although bearing twice the usual weight would in time weary their steeds, they could make better time this way.

Every time he had a chance, Doc Harbin studied the ancient dish with the aid of his powerful lens. During the second rest stop, he drew Brant aside to confer. The old scientist seemed agitated, as if suppressing a discovery of considerable interest.

"Can you read the old writing yet, Doc?" inquired Brant. The other man shook his head.

"I can only make out, or guess the meaning of, about one word in four," he confessed. "Nevertheless, Jim, I think I've discovered something that may help us."

"Well, we could sure use a little help right now, so let me have it," said Brant. Harbin produced the worn and ancient dish.

"The charactery inscribed around the lip of the dish is too ancient and too illegible for me to figure out, lacking my library and my instruments," Will Harbin admitted. "But this design in the central part, this wandering, curved line, seemed utterly meaningless until it occurred to me to compare it to my maps."

He paused impressively, but Brant was in no mood for a build-up.

"Spit it out, Doc," he grunted.

"Very well! This curved line matches quite closely the contours of the edge of the prehistoric continent whose cliffwall, or shoreline, we are now following," he said. Brant looked unimpressed.

"So what? A map—what of it?"

Will Harbin pointed to a place on the meandering line graven in the golden dish.

"This spot lies about two hours' hard ride south from where we are now," he said excitedly. "There is a bit of writing etched at this point—see?"

Brant nodded briefly. "So what? If you can't read the writing—"

"These characters are almost legible," breathed Harbin. "They translate as something in the nature of 'the refuge,' or 'the way in,' or 'the safe place,'—I can't be precisely sure—"

Brant shrugged irritably. "So what does it mean, d'you think? C'mon, Doc, we're wasting time."

Harbin looked dubious. "I'm not exactly sure . . . a cavern, perhaps, a hiding place, some sort of niche in the cliffwall important enough, or secure enough, to be so marked. It is the only place on the ancient map that is marked at all."

Brant rubbed the line of his jaw with one thumbnail, thinking.

"A hiding place, then. God, we could use one! But will it still be there, after half a million years, or however old this map may be?"

"I can't say," Harbin admitted. "But it's better than running. Because they have more men than we, and probably more guns. And sooner or later, our lopers will founder under the double weight. . . ."

"I know, damn the luck," growled Brant. "Okay, since it's in our path, we'll watch for it. Let me know when the map exactly matches the terrain."

"I will," said the other man.

They mounted up and rode on into the day.

Zuarra shared the saddle with Brant on the remainder of that day's riding, and she seemed to be in a surly and sullen mood. Glancing back, Brant guessed the reason. For Agila had the other woman, Suoli, before him in the saddle, and his hands were wandering under her robes and he was whispering something in her ear that caused her to giggle and to blush shyly.

Hearing the giggling, Zuarra tightened her jaw and pinched her full lips together, staring ahead grimly.

Brant grinned wolfishly, but said nothing. His arms tightened a little about Zuarra's lissom waist, and she did not seemingly resent the minor intimacy.

The breach between the two "sisters" had widened since that episode on the ledge where the more feminine of the two had fearfully shrunk from coming to Zuarra's aid. Brant kept his thoughts to himself, but enjoyed the tantalizing nearness of the woman in his arms and savored the dry, musky perfume of her body.

They rode on into the unknown, for there was nothing else to do, since to stand and fight against Tuan's band, which now numbered at least fourteen warriors, would have been, quite simply, suicidal. But inwardly Brant felt a welling-up of hopelessness: they were following a map millions of years old, perhaps, looking for a refuge which might very well no longer exist.

But there was nothing else to do. . . .

During the next rest stop, Brant scanned the ridgeline through his binoculars, and found the tireless riders. He swore under his breath.

"They keep up with us, the bastards, but nothing more! Why, goddammit, *why?*"

It was a rhetorical question, but Will Harbin took it seriously enough to offer an answer.

"Possibly because Tuan fears that, if pressed, we will destroy the golden dish," he suggested. "We could do it very easily, you know. One bolt from your power guns would fuse the ancient relic to a shapeless puddle of metal. . . ."

Brant considered. "Hmmm . . . hadn't thought of that. You may be right. You're a good man to have along, Doc, on a risky ride like this one."

Harbin smiled and said nothing.

*   *   *

Just past midday, they reached the site marked on the golden map. Or so, at least, Harbin was convinced.

"The weather on Mars is of little consequence," he said. "It takes many millions of years to sufficiently deface a shoreline like the one we are following. The site marked on the map is—there!"

He pointed to a narrow cleft in the wall. It looked so unimportant that Brant would easily have ridden past it without even noticing it. His expression was dubious.

"You sure, Doc?" Harbin nodded.

"Sure as I can be."

They rode closer. Harbin gave voice to an exclamation, and pointed with a trembling hand. Brant peered and saw ancient characters cut in the stone above the cleft, almost worn to the point of being indistinguishable.

"Can you read 'em?" Brant demanded gruffly.

The expression on Doc's homely face became somber, almost reverential. "No, but I can almost guess," he breathed.

13
The Safe Place

Dismounting, and leading their riding beasts by the bridles, they entered the narrow cleft in single file, with Brant leading the way. Harbin studied the rock formations of the walls, and remarked that all of this was exceptionally ancient.

"But it's obviously been improved upon by man," he muttered, pointing. "See? There and there? Chisel-work: someone has widened this passage where it narrowed, and the ceiling overhead has been groined where necessary, but a more stable roofing."

Brant nodded curtly. "Wonder how far back this cleft goes?" he mused aloud.

"Let's find out," suggested Harbin.

They went deeper and deeper into the solid bedrock of the ancient continent. The women seemed uncertain and nervous. Finally, Zuarra stepped to where Brant walked in the lead.

"What is it, woman?"

"Should not we have posted a guard at the entrance?" Zuarra asked. Brant looked at her, then grinned.

"We're looking for 'a safe place,' " he said shortly. "If we find it, we won't need a guard. If we don't, then we'll go back and post one." He chuckled and she gazed at him inquiringly.

"Probably Agila," Brant grinned. "He's the one we can most comfortably do without!"

At that remark, she, too, smiled, rather vindictively. He

gathered that she would have been all too pleased if they had abandoned the lean wolf at any point of this journey.

They went on, exploring the narrow-walled cavern.

Harbin examined the walls as they went past, pointing out where hands—presumably human—had widened and smoothed out the narrower or rougher portion places.

"Notice the chisel-work?" he asked, pointing.

"Yeah," Brant grunted. "Also, see how the floor is pretty smooth underfoot?"

"I've noticed," said the older man.

"Wonder why anybody'd take the trouble to do this," mused Brant curiously. "Suppose people lived in here once?"

Will Harbin shrugged. "Hard to tell . . . but if they did, it was ages ago and whatever signs of their residence they left—smoke from cookfires, for instance, gnawed bones, refuse, broken crockery—have long since been obliterated by the passage of time."

Brant privately guessed that the long, narrow cavern had been the tomb of a clan prince, or the hiding place for a treasure trove. Or, just possibly both. There had to be *something* about the cave that made it a place of very special importance —or why else would its precise location be so carefully engraved into the ancient dish of pallid Martian gold?

He mentioned these notions in low tones to Harbin, not wishing the others to overhear. The People had certain scruples about plundering the burial-places of their kingly dead, and, while Agila was not likely to object to picking up some ancient loot—thief that he already admittedly was—the women might not have been of the same mind.

"Those possibilities also occurred to me," nodded the old scientist. "But this does not resemble any of the native tombs or sepulchers I know of. Well, maybe we'll find out. . . ."

They went on into the gloom.

After a time, they came to the end of the cavern, and found something odd and unexpected. It was neither a coffin nor a cache, however, but something neither of the two Earthsiders could possibly have predicted.

It was . . . a door!

A stone archway, at any rate, sealed with a gigantic slab of dull metal. The two looked at each other blankly.

By the light of his fluoro, Harbin closely scrutinized the surface of the metal. He uttered an exclamation and dazedly mumbled something under his breath. It was in no language with which Brant had any familiarity.

"What did you say, Doc?" he inquired.

Harbin looked at him a bit bemusedly.

"Nothing, really. That inscription—see it, here and here? Almost worn away by time . . ."

"Yeah, I see it," said Brant. "But it's in the Tongue, and what you said was in some other language."

Harbin smiled faintly. "You're right, Jim! It was Italian, of the Middle Ages. Did you ever read the ancient poet Dante?"

Brant wrinkled up his brow. "*Paradise Lost*?" he made a guess. Ancient literature was not something he was very fond of.

Harbin shook his head. "Close, but not quite it. No . . . the *Divine Comedy*. An epic about a sort of guided tour of Heaven, Hell, and Purgatory, you might say."

"I don't get it," admitted Brant.

"This inscription reminded me of the one Dante said was carved over the gates of Hell . . . '*Abandon hope, all ye who enter here*' . . ."

The words echoed solemnly in the silent gloom. Here in this stark and lifeless place, they sounded even more ominous than they would have under the open sky and in the light of day. Zuarra repressed a shudder of . . . of what? Perhaps it was foreboding.

"Shall we not discover what lies hidden beyond the portal?" suggested Agila. "It might be a great treasure."

"It might, indeed," said Will Harbin absently. And then he added, to himself: "Or a great mystery. . . ."

Brant examined the portal, with its ominous inscription. He could see no lock, but when he tested his strength against it, it gave only a little.

"If I didn't know better, I'd say it was bolted from the other side," he said incredulously.

"Well, Jim, how do you know it isn't?" asked Harbin. The strange nature of their discovery intrigued him more and more—and scientists of his persuasion develop lively curiosities.

"Because we're deep into the solid bedrock of the continent by this point, and there's certainly no way out," Brant answered him gruffly. "What did they do, lock themselves in there to die?"

"I don't know," replied the older man. "But I'm getting very interested in finding out. Do you think we can get the door open?"

Brant shrugged. "I suppose so. There are the hinges, and with a narrow beam we could cut them through and pry the door out of its frame with the right tools, bolt or no bolt. But it would take some doing. . . ."

"Then we had better get started," the scientist remarked. "For our friends are not going to stay up on the ridgeline for very long, now that they can see we have found a refuge."

"Yeah," Brant agreed soberly, "it's either that, or hold them off at the mouth of the cave. It's narrow enough for one man to hold it against many . . . but I'd kinda like to see what's behind that door, first. I like to know what's at my back in a fight like this."

They began working on the metal door.

Zuarra said nothing, but in her thoughts echoed that grim, enigmatic phrase the old man had spoken.

What good thing could you expect to find behind a door marked with a warning like "Abandon hope, all ye who enter here"?

14
Behind the Door

With Agila at his side, Brant began working on the portal. The others withdrew to the middle section of the narrow cave, with Will Harbin and Zuarra keeping watch at the cave mouth against the expected arrival of the outlaw band.

Adjusting his power gun to the narrowest setting, Brant aimed a needle-beam at the topmost hinge. Sparks flew crackling in all directions, illuminating the dark cavern with an eerie blue-white glare.

The metal glowed with heat and began gradually to soften. The heat at the far end of the cavern became at first uncomfortable, then hard to endure. Brant withdrew, gesturing curtly to Agila to take up the work, and turned down the controls on his suit.

Before long, he turned the heat off entirely and even unseamed the insulated garment from throat to navel. By this time, Agila had stripped naked save for a cloth wound about his loins. His coppery-red body glistened with oily perspiration.

Brant replaced him and let him withdraw to cooler parts of the cavern. They had cut entirely through the topmost hinge by this time, and Brant began working on the midmost hinge.

There was no real danger that this work would exhaust the power cells in the pistol, for they automatically recharged themselves by the use of dialetric accumulators, as did the pressure-still and the heating elements in the insulated suits the two Earthsiders wore. But it was hot, nasty work, the air reeking with ozone and stinking of hot, dripping metal.

Brant persevered. When he turned the job over to Agila,

and strolled to the entrance of the cave to cool off, Harbin greeted him cheerfully.

"No sign of our friends yet, Jim. How's the work going?"

"Almost done," Brant grunted, sucking in lungfuls of clean, cold, pure air. "Doc, I'm gonna need that geologist's pick you use for cutting fossils out of the rocks. Need something to help pry the door loose, once we got the three hinges cut through."

"Certainly. The pick is in my saddlebags. You take over here, and I'll find it for you." The scientist went to where the lopers lay curled in fitful slumber and began rummaging through his baggage.

Left alone with Zuarra, Brant glanced at the woman.

"You all right?" he inquired gruffly. "Not frightened, are you?"

She leveled a scornful glance at him, then relented, smiling a little. He had not noticed what a lovely smile she had until just now. Her teeth were white and even in her copper mask of a face.

"Only a fool or a madman would not feel a little frightened in such a place, O Brant, with enemies nigh upon us and nowhere left to run. But Zuarra is not so frightened that she cannot maintain her vigilance!"

He patted her on the shoulder. "Good girl," he said heavily.

A short while later, Agila yelled in an excited voice from the back of the cave. None of them could quite make out what the lean wolf said, but all could easily guess the meaning of his cry, drowned in booming echoes as it was in that narrow space between walls of solid rock.

The third and last hinge was cut through, Brant guessed. And he was right.

Using the point of the pick for leverage, and wedging their fingertips into the slight cranny between the edge of the metal door and the rock into which it was set, the two half-naked men toiled like demons in the glare of Harbin's light. The job was rendered much more difficult than it would otherwise

have been, because the metal door was fiercely hot to the
touch in places.

But it got done, that job, and the portal came loose.
Holding the light high, Harbin was the first to peer within the
black opening and to discover what might lie behind the
portal that had been sealed and forgotten so many eons
before. He uttered a dazed exclamation.

"What d'you see, Doc?" Brant demanded. The older man
handed him the light, stepping out of the way.

"Look for yourself, Jim," he breathed excitedly.

It was a stair.

A narrow stair, cut out of the bedrock of the continent,
winding down and down, to unguessable depths of black
mystery below.

Drowned in a darkness deeper than the gloom of Erebus or
Hades itself was that ancient, winding stair. What might be
waiting discovery in the Stygian deeps below where they
stood none of them could imagine. But *something* was down
there, that was for certain—or else, why cut those steps into
the stone at all, or seal the thing up with a metal door?

Brant said as much to Doc, who nodded. The three natives
took a look in turn, Agila hungrily, greedy for treasure, Suoli
timidly, eyes wide, Zuarra boldly, but warily. No matter how
they held the light, or directed its beam, all they could see
was the stone stair going down and down. After thirty steps,
there was a square stone platform. Then the stair turned at an
angle to continue into the depths.

They could see as far as seven platforms down, before the
light failed them.

"Two hundred and ten steps, at least," muttered Brant.
"That's gotta be a good two hundred feet down under the
surface. And God knows how far down the stair goes. But—
why? And—to *what?*"

"There's only one way to find out, my boy!" said Doc
jubilantly. Brant grinned at him understandingly. The excitement and enthusiasm in the older man's face made him look
absurdly youthful, even boyish.

"Yeah . . . I know," he muttered. "I got an itch so see
what's at the bottom of the stair, too. But what are we gonna

do about the lopers? We sure can't lead them down the stair, and there's no food for them in the cave. Of course, we could unsaddle them and take off their bits and bridles and turn 'em loose. On their own, they'd have no trouble finding food along the edges of the cliff . . . but that would mean, when we came back to the surface, we'd have to go afoot from here on."

"I know, I know!" Harbin burst out impatiently. "I'm not trying to suggest we all make the descent, just one or two of us! Of course, that would be a little unfair, because if we're going to be in a fight with those people following us, it would leave the defenders short-handed. . . ."

Brant grinned sourly. "Well, we could hardly be more short-handed than we are right now," he pointed out. "And look how few guns we have between us, as it is!"

"So what do you suggest we do, Jim?" inquired the other.

Brant chuckled and clapped a big hand on his thin shoulder. "Aw, hell, Doc, you're dyin' to find out what's down there, so you go ahead. Here—take one of my guns and leave the rifles with us. We'll be able to hold 'em off when they come. Suoli won't amount to anything, sure, but I'll bet Zuarra is a dead shot."

Will Harbin didn't need much more urging. They bade him good-bye for a time, wished him luck, and watched as the older man, lighting his way before him, started down the stone stair.

He went down and down, dwindling from view. After a while, even the light from his lamp was merely a spark, dim and faint, in the Stygian darkness.

Then they returned to where Suoli was standing guard at the mouth of the cave. There still was no sign of the men who had been following them, but Brant felt inwardly certain that by now they had all descended to the foot of the cliff and were not very far away. Probably, they were even at that moment watching the entrance of the cave from places of concealment, and debating between themselves whether to try to rush the entrance or ask for a parley.

Time had almost run out for them, Brant knew. And he

rather wished he was on the stair with Harbin at that moment, and not crouching here, awaiting a battle. . . .

Whoever the unknown hands had been who shaped the stair, they had been superb masons, for the stonework was cut to a nicety. On earth, the steps would have been foul and slick with moss or mold or lichen in these subterranean depths, but here on Mars, where any kind of moisture was rarer than rubies and far more precious than pearls, such flora could not survive, and the steps were dry and clean underfoot.

Doc Harbin went down the first three or four levels before he had to rest and catch his breath and rub the beginning of stiffness from the muscles of his calves. He took a sip of water from the sealed canteen, rose to his feet, and continued the descent.

There was something so boring about the trip down that even his curiosity began to diminish after a time. There was nothing to see except naked stone walls and platforms and steps, which were all exactly the same to look at. He had been hoping for inscriptions, even graffiti, but found nothing.

And the silence was—as the saying goes—deafening. There was not the slightest sound, other than the rasp of his bootheels against smooth, dry rock and the wheeze of his breathing. Still, he toiled on. There was a mystery here, and Will Harbin was determined to seek it out. . . .

He had been keeping careful mental notes of the number of platforms he passed. After he had reached the tenth such, and knew that he was now well below the most distant part of the stair which they had been able to see from the doorway above, he stopped taking count and just plodded grimly down, and down, and down.

Then he became aware of something a little odd. The air was *warmer* than seemed natural . . . or was it the exertion? As Brant had done earlier, while cutting through the hinges with his power gun, Harbin turned down the heat-control of his suit, and eventually turned it off altogether. Before long, he unseamed his protective suit to the belly.

After a while, something else equally strange came gradually to his notice. It was so very unlikely, that at first he dismissed it from his mind as sheer imagination. Erelong, he was forced to admit that it was, after all, a fact.

The air was getting more humid the farther down he climbed.

Now this was, if not impossible, at least very mysterious. The slowly rising temperatures could be understood if you considered that the farther down beneath the planet's surface he went, the nearer he came to whatever volcanic heat might still be lingering in the core of the ancient planet. And heat, trapped in this stone well, sealed for uncountable ages by that metal door, would have no place to go. But *humidity*—that was quite another thing.

There was no reason for the humidity, or, at least, none that he could think of.

But before long he was forced to recognize its existence as a simple fact. Resting his aching legs on a platform, he saw patches of *dampness* on the stone wall directly in front of him. He might not have noticed the phenomenon had it not been for the angle at which his lamp was set, which made the moisture glisten.

"Damndest thing!" the old man said to himself.

He rose after a time and continued down the stair, limping stiffly, staggering with fatigue, wondering if he would not be wise to pause for a nap at the next platform.

He did so, and let exhaustion drift him into slumber from which he woke, after an indeterminate time, to yawn and stretch, feeling every stiff and sore muscle his body possessed, each a clear and distinct pang.

"Not so young as I used to be," he grunted to himself, trying to massage some of the stiffness out of his legs, at least.

He wondered how far down he had come by this point. It could easily have been a full mile, perhaps even more. He inwardly cursed himself for carelessly losing count of the total platforms he had reached and passed.

It had gotten so warm and humid by now, that he decided to remove the heatsuit entirely; it was lightweight nioflex and could easily be rolled up and thrust under his equipment belt. Under the suit he wore the usual one-piece garment called a liner, much the same sort of thing that spacemen wore under their insulated airsuits.

"There, that's a little better!" he said to himself, wishing he had something wherewith to mop the perspiration from his face and throat. But handkerchiefs are seldom found on the desert world, where the air is so desiccated that people rarely perspire for any reason.

He limped and stumbled slowly down another six or seven flights of the stair, resting now at each platform as he reached it, and before long stretched out to sleep again.

When he awoke, quite suddenly, and with his pulses rising in alarm, he did not at once realize what had startled him to wakefulness.

A moment or two later, the sound came again, and he gasped in sheer amazement.

Human voices.

15

On the Stair

At first, the old scientist could not tell whether the voices came from above him, or from below, for the echoes that bounced from wall to wall not only rendered the voices incomprehensible, but made their source unguessable.

With his back against the wall of the platform, and one of Brant's power guns in his fist, Will Harbin waited with a pounding heart to see what was going to happen.

Before long, he relaxed with a deep, heartfelt sigh. For the voices, he now discerned, came from above, and one of them was calling "Doc! Doc?" hoarsely.

"I'm down here, Jim," he shouted back. "Just keep coming."

In time they hobbled down to where he sat resting, Brant in the lead, helping a pale and staggering Zuarra, with the villainous Agila in the rear, helping along little Suoli. If one of his hands was furtively squeezing her plump breasts, she seemed too weary to object to the surreptitious caress.

They joined him on the platform, glad of another chance to rest their aching muscles. Looking his friends over, Will Harbin observed that they had endured the same changes in temperature and humidity that he had noticed, for all had stripped—Brant to ragged briefs, Agila to his loincloth, and the women had removed everything. All three were slick with oily sweat, but the natives seemed to have suffered more than had Brant.

This made sense to the scientist. After all, both he and Brant had been born and raised on Earth and were accustomed to a denser, warmer, damper, more oxygen-rich atmosphere than were the Martians. The two Earthsiders had undergone certain series of medical treatments, including surgical implants, which adjusted their lungs to the thinner, colder air and their metabolism to conditions on the surface of Mars. Akin to thermostats, these devices were self-regulating, and had now, probably, shut down, since the air was warm and moist and rich in oxygen.

But the natives were thoroughly unaccustomed to these conditions, and were suffering. Stubborn children of a hardy race, they would erelong become acclimated, but it would take some time, he knew.

Resting on the platform, Harbin and Brant compared notes.

"What happened up above?" inquired Harbin. "Did Tuan and his band turn up?"

"They did that," Brant grunted ruefully. "And we had to back off, they had so much firepower we couldn't even get near enough to the mouth of the cave to return their fire."

"So—what happened?"

"Since there wasn't any cover in the cave, we came out the back door and down the stair, looking for you."

"Do you think the outlaws will follow?" asked Harbin.

Brant shrugged. "Hard to say . . . maybe they're just superstitious enough to shy away from this: you know how they fear and venerate the Ancients and their remains and ruins. Anyway, Agila and I got the metal door back in place and fused it with the lasers. That's better than nothing."

Will harbin nodded soberly. It wasn't much to pin their hopes on, but Brant was right: it *was* better than nothing.

Just barely.

Brant was unhappy at having to turn and run for it, but there hadn't been any other viable choice. It also griped him that they had been forced to abandon the lopers, most of the gear, even the tents. They had only brought along the food stores, the weapons, and garments. And now, in this tepid, moist air, even the clothing could have been left behind, except that who could have imagined they'd find heat and moisture down here, so far below the surface?

The one thing Will Harbin had neglected to bring along with him on his descent was a supply of food, so once they were rested and somewhat refreshed, they dug into the chow. It was rude fare, cold meat and the like, which couldn't even be heated, but when you're tired and hungry, even cold meat tastes delicious.

Munching sliced meat, Brant remembered one thing he had forgotten to mention.

"One thing may help slow 'em down a little," he grunted. "I left the gold dish behind, right in front of the door we sealed up behind us. If that's all they really want, it might stop 'em. Anyway, it seemed like a good idea at the time!"

"That's good thinking, Jim. The writing on the door might scare them off, too. They won't know what it means, probably, unless they've got a renegade priest with them, but it should make them a bit more wary and cautious."

Brant grinned. "Yeah, they can guess it means more 'keep off the grass,' " he said jokingly.

"More along the line of 'beware of the dragon,' I'd say," Harbin quipped. They chuckled. It felt good to laugh again. Somehow, both men felt the worst part of this was over.

They couldn't have been more wrong, of course.

They continued the descent again, after resting. After all, there was nothing else to do and nowhere else to go, and they were all consumed by curiosity to find out what lay at the bottom of the interminable stair, which would have to explain why it had been built so many ages ago, and at such a price in human toil.

The farther down they went, the warmer grew the air, ever richer in oxygen. Since they were climbing down at what might well be described at little better than a snail's pace, the slowness of their descent gave the three natives a chance to adapt to these amazing new conditions, somewhat in the manner of a deep-sea diver back on Earth who avoids the bends by coming up to the surface very slowly.

Zuarra and Agila were the first to recover, for they were strong and hardened, both of them, while poor little Suoli lacked those qualities, as well as courage and stamina. Brant noticed they were constantly together, Agila and Suoli, snuggling together when it was time to sleep, and whispering in each other's ear, which made Suoli giggle like a schoolgirl.

Zuarra girmly ignored this, and clung to the side of Brant. He figured that it would not be long before Agila and Suoli became lovers, if they were not at that stage already, and readied himself for trouble.

Very often Brant helped Zuarra down with an arm around her waist, and more than once he found Zuarra gazing at him with a strange, indefinable expression in her lovely emerald eyes. When discovered looking at him, the tall woman would glance away quickly, and very often she would blush and even bite her lip.

When they rested at each platform, she sat very near to him and often, seemingly by accident, her naked knee or bare thigh would be pressed against his. She seemed unaware of this bodily contact, but Brant had a feeling she was quite aware of it and was doing it deliberately: what he didn't know was her reason.

Was it to demonstrate her indifference to Suoli's cuddling and giggling with Agila, or, perhaps, an attempt to make her former "sister" jealous by seeming to be infatuated with the big Earthsider?

He shrugged, and put the question out of his mind. Sooner or later it would probably come out, and, anyway, there was no trying to understand women. He had never had much luck figuring out the women of his own kind back home on Earth, so why should he even try understanding the moods and motives of a foreign woman on a distant planet?

As if the warmth and moisture were not strange enough, before very long a new enigma presented itself.

Light shone from below.

It was a dim glow, to be sure, but it *was* light: very welcome in the pitch-darkness of the stair, for even despite the light shed by their lamp, the gloom was all about, and hovered near, and depressed their spirits.

It was not the ruddy light you could expect to be shed by volcanic fires or pools of molten lava, either, but something quite different—a wan, pearly luminance such as none of them had ever seen before, softer than the cold moonlight of the distant Earth, and dimmer than the radiance of day.

They sensed that they were quite close to the bottom of the stair by now, for not only was the strange light visible, but the air was fresher and was quickening with a gentle, welcome breeze.

Weary to the point of exhaustion, they rested again, and fed on the last scraps, and fell asleep. All but Will Harbin. Although he was as weary as any of them, doubtless, his scientific curiosity had roused itself again. He was determined that the discovery would be his alone, and that he would be the first to find whatever it was had lain hidden here for ages, buried in the bowels of the ancient planet. Careful not to awaken his companions, Doc rose and stole limping down the stair and into the growing light.

A time later, Brant roused himself with a grunt and noticed that the old scientist was missing.

"Crazy fool, sneaking off alone, when none of us knows what danger we may find at the bottom!" he growled, cursing and waking up Agila and the women.

They went down the stair, and, quite suddenly, they came to the bottom of it. The passage turned at a sharp angle and then opened into a doorway, on whose broad stoop Will Harbin was sitting, staring about with wonder in his face.

The four stopped abruptly as if petrified in their tracks. Their eyes widened incredulously, jaws dropped open, and Zuarra clutched at Brant's arm, as they stared upon a secret locked away from the world for unknown ages. . . .

Far above where they stood, Tuan also stood staring. He was staring at the metal door which shielded the secret stair from the knowledge of men.

"The thief could only have gone this way, O Tuan, for there is no other path to follow. He and his accomplices, the hated *f'yagha*, will be crouching behind that door, besoiling themselves with fear!"

"Mayhap," growled Tuan. He and his warriors had lingered for what must have been hours, cautiously watching for any sign of activity within the cave, before venturing therein, only to find it devoid of any living thing save for the lopers, hissing with terror, who had retreated from their fire to the farthest reaches of the cave.

It was not that he was not brave, this Tuan, but the cave—dark and narrow—made a perfect trap, should any of the Hated Ones remain alive. And prudence—caution—was a quality which a chieftain learned to develop early on in his career or that career seldom lasted very long. And you do not go charging by ones and twos into the very teeth of the enemy, presenting a tempting target as you do so, silhouetted against the day.

"Mayhap," he repeated thoughtfully. Tuan, once a princeling of the Dragon Moon nation, was a tall, lithe, broad-shouldered man, lean and tough and sinewy, with cold green eyes and a hard mouth.

"There is some writing there, O Tuan!" muttered another, pointing. It was in the Old Speech, and none of them could read it. But they knew in their hearts that it was a warning of some kind.

"What shall we do, my chief?" asked another, a one-eyed rogue called Asouk. "We have the sacred dish, safely returned to us. . . ."

"We shall see what lies beyond the door," growled Tuan. "Break it down, O Naruth," he said, speaking to the burliest of his outlaws. "Use the power guns if it be sealed or barred from behind."

They broke through the door erelong and found the hidden stair. Muttering and signing themselves superstitiously, they peered down the winding stair into the ultimate blackness of the pit.

"What now, O Kiridh?" demanded Tuan. "The dogs are not cowering and wetting themselves in terror, as you said."

The man called Kiridh blinked stolidly in the face of this small rebuke.

"That is for my chief to say," he muttered. Scratching his jaw with one thumbnail, Tuan considered. Then:

"We descend the stair," he grunted.

IV

~~~~~~~~~

DOWN THERE

16
Many Marvels

At first, the travelers looked down. From the edge of the stone stoop where Doc Harbin sat, the ground declined in a gentle slope. The slope was thickly carpeted with tightly curled and interwoven moss of an amazing color, or variety of shades, which ranged from peacock blue to metallic azure to deepest indigo.

It was moist and beaded with dew, the moss that grew like a living carpet, and starred all over with tiny white flowers. They exchanged glances of utter amazement, especially Agila and the women. For, while Harbin and Brant had seen such moss carpeting back earthside (although perhaps not of the same amazing color), the Martians had never imagined such a sight.

Will Harbin had removed his boots and was working his toes blissfully in the dewy moss, much as a small boy might wriggle his bare toes in the deliciously damp grass of a meadow.

The dim opalescent luminance was everywhere, brighter than moonlight back earthside, but only a shade dimmer than the wan daylight of the Desert World. It seemed sourceless and omnipresent and cast no discernible shadows.

Brant looked up, to discover another marvel. The sky was dark, so dark that you could hardly see the rocky roof of the enormous cavern in which they found themselves. And enormous was the word—it seemed to go on for miles.

"Doc, just how big *is* this place?" asked Brant in awed, hushed tones. The older man shrugged.

"Hard to say: couple of hundred square miles, at least. Cavern's too huge to be artificial; must have formed when the planet was molten and plastic—huge gas bubble got trapped beneath the surface and hardened. Mars is smaller than Earth, you know, and cooled a heck of a lot faster."

"Yeah," Brant nodded. "Also has a lot less gravity. Back home, the sheer weight of the continent above it would have made this place collapse early on."

"Quite right," mused Harbin. He seemed beside himself with delight at having discovered what must surely have been the most astounding of all the many mysteries of Mars.

Brant looked down the mossy slope to see what lay beyond, but a range of low hills blocked the distance from his view. Then Zuarra clutched his bare arm, pointing.

"What—what are *those*, O Brant?" she whispered.

He looked away to the right, in the direction the woman had indicated, and saw to his further amazement something remarkably like a forest. But it was not a forest of trees, or like anything he had ever seen before. . . .

It was a forest of tall, spongy things that looked for all the world like mushrooms or toadstools. But even back home, mushrooms had never to his knowledge grown so huge. Many of them were four or five feet high, but some stood as tall as ten or twelve.

Suoli gasped and clapped her hands with delight at the fungus forest. Even Brant had to admire the brilliant colors, and let his eyes feast on their delicious variety. The fungus growths were of every shade from chalk white to rich cream, canary yellow, tangerine, umber, rust brown. And they were spotted or striped or splotched with vivid green, rich crimson, purple and vermilion.

The Martians drank in the view delightedly. And this was only natural, since their dreary world offered so little by way of color or contrast upon which to feed the eye. Little more than red sand, slate gray rock, and dully purple sky.

Brant looked questioningly at Harbin, but the other man shook his head simply.

"Don't ask me, Jim! We've never even found fossil records of anything like that, and precious little fossil vegetation of any description," he said. "But, then, after all, we've only been here on Mars for a few generations, and it took us centuries to compile a fossil record of Earth, and even it's still not complete."

Brant made no reply, save for a slight, cynical smile. The Colonial Administration here on Mars, like most of the governments back earthside, were probably equally reluctant to expend any funds to support something as obviously unprofitable as fossil-hunting. . . .

Zuarra slipped her small, strong hand into Brant's big paw and gently urged him in the direction of the fungus-forest. He followed, wanting a closer look at the huge, nodding stalks with their bulbous heads, and the others trailed behind. Following Harbin's example, Brant removed his boots to enjoy the dewy carpet of moss under his bare feet.

Closer, they paused to breathe in the odd aroma of the forest. There was a muskiness that was not at all unpleasant, together with a sweetish-sour smell like cream that has turned, but there was also an indescribable scent that made Brant's mouth water hungrily. It was something like the smell of fresh, hot gingerbread, and a little like hot buttered popcorn— neither of which he had tasted for many years.

"Suppose these things are edible?" he inquired of Harbin, who had followed them across the mossy lawn.

"I've no idea," Harbin confessed. "No sign of animal life as yet, but if there *is* any to be discovered, it must feed on *something*. Look there—in fact, I believe something has been feeding on the mushrooms!"

He pointed to shallow gouges and dry pock-marks on the surface of the nearer growths. The marks reminded Brant uncannily of the bare patches on saplings, where hungry deer in winter have gnawed away strips of bark.

Just then, as chance would have it, their guessing was confirmed. For something remarkably like a dragonfly came whizzing through the air in their direction.

It certainly looked like a dragonfly, with its long, tubular body and stiff, thrumming wings like sheeted mica. But Brant had never heard of a dragonfly as long as a grown man's arm, and sporting a wingspread of what must have been seven feet or more.

It flashed through the air toward them, and the sound of its flight was clearly audible—something about midway between the whine of a rifle bullet and the whistle of an arrow.

As they stared, the gorgeous winged creature alighted on one of the nearer mushrooms, and sank a long proboscis into the flesh of the fungus and began sucking greedily.

"O, how beautiful!" exclaimed Zuarra, clasping her hands together between her ripe breasts.

Brant had to agree. The torso of the insect was a gorgeous red-gold, the vibrant wings were veined with metallic azure, and glinted in the dim light like thin slices of opal. Its eyes were gemmy clusters of glistening black crystals.

A moment or two later, the thing whizzed off, leaving a small puncture in the side of the mushroom, which oozed a colorless sap. Doc cautiously dabbled his fingers in the sticky stuff, and sniffed it suspiciously. It smelled very much like apple cider, he decided. And was sour-sweet to the taste, when he touched a drop to the tip of his tongue.

"Careful, Doc!" exclaimed Brant. "Back earthside, you know, some of these things are good food, but others are deadly poisonous."

"I know," smiled Harbin, staring around dreamily. "But somehow I tend to doubt it . . . hard to believe anything in this beautiful garden could be dangerous or deadly . . . it's like Eden before the Serpent. . . ."

They wandered deeper into the weird forest of giant fungi, Brant and Zuarra, and Agila and Suoli, naked and hand in hand—which reinforced Will Harbin's comparison of this place to the fabled Garden of Eden. Nothing that they saw looked harmful: small crimson things like beetles scuttled and burrowed into the indigo moss, and tunneled into the dried stalks of the fallen giants; something as richly colored as a hummingbird, and of about the same size, whizzed by on all-but-invisible wings. When it alighted on a fallen fungus trunk they realized it looked more like a huge fly than a hummingbird, after all.

Harbin remarked that, insofar as the fossil record had

proven, Mars had never supported avian life, either bird or insect. The winged serpents of Martian legend he dismissed out of hand as being that—merely legend.

"Where d'you suppose all of this light is coming from?" muttered Brant. "Not from the sky. Seems to be from the surface—see how brilliant it is beyond those hills?"

"Yep. Well . . . let's take a look," suggested Harbin. "Only way to find out for sure. May be in the very air itself, chemical phosphorescence—"

Brant cut him off with an abrupt gesture. He opened his mouth to yell a warning, but it was already too late. Agila had broken off a dripping chunk of the soft underflesh of one of the huge toadstools and was gingerly nibbling on it. Harbin uttered an exclamation, but Brant stopped his protest with an easy shrug.

"We'll soon find out if the stuff is bad to eat," he grinned. "What the hell, we can do without that treacherous devil to watch."

But he warned Suoli not to taste the stuff, and strolled near to take a look. It was yellow and soft, like spongecake, and dripping like a fresh honeycomb.

"How does it taste?" he inquired.

"Very good!" mumbled Agila around a cheekful. "A taste such as Agila has never before encountered."

He was lapping the stuff up as fast as he could claw another handful out of the soft trunk, and it didn't seem to be making him sick, so Brant cautiously tasted a crumb of it himself.

It was sweet as honey and as tangy as wine, the dripping fluid, and the meat bore a distinct flavor of applesauce.

Just then a call came from some little distance away. Brant turned to see that, while he had gone to check out Agila's reaction to the fungus, Harbin had continued on to climb the gentle slope of the hills, hoping to discover the source of the illumination.

"Anything to see, Doc?" Brant called back.

For a moment, Harbin made no reply, staring raptly into the distance. Then he turned to beckon to Brant, and the expression on his face was one such as Brant had never before seen, save perhaps in religious paintings of prophets and saints caught up in ecstasy.

"You must see this, my boy . . . a miracle beyond belief."

17

Beyond Belief

Leaving Zuarra, who was cautiously sampling the fleshy meat of the great fungus growths, Brant climbed the mossy slope of the hill to where Will Harbin stood awestruck, staring with wondering gaze into the luminosity.

And Brant stopped short, uttering a grunt of amazement.

From a gemmy shore at the foot of the other side of the hill, for as far as the eye could reach, there stretched a shining sea.

The water was milky-white, quite opaque, and was clearly the source of the mysterious luminance, for the radiant fluid was like the essence of light itself, curdled into pearly fire.

"A . . . *sea*," whispered Brant faintly. "Here at the bottom of the world . . . !"

"Yes. In fact, it is the Last Ocean," said Will Harbin softly. "The last of all the mighty oceans of primal Mars, draining into this cavern and forgotten since the beginning of time itself . . . what a marvel. A miracle!"

They stood for a moment, staring in awe at the vast expanse of luminous waters, and Doc Harbin murmured something in low tones to himself, his expression bemused and wondering. Brant glanced at him inquiringly.

"More Dante?" Harbin flushed a little, and grinned.

"No, a British poet this time—Coleridge." And he repeated a few lines of the old poem.

> " '. . . where Alph the sacred river ran
> Through caverns measureless to man,
> Down to a sunless sea . . .' "

*   *   *

Brant grunted, impressed. "You'd almost think he got a glimpse of this place, somehow," he remarked.

"Maybe he did, in some uncanny way," Harbin mused. "He said he wrote the poem in a dream, and, when awake, copied down as many lines as he could still remember."

"What . . . makes it glow like that?" Brant wondered.

"Natural phosphorescence, maybe. Some luminous chemical. Even algae, just possibly. Or residual radiation," murmured Doc Harbin. "Anyway, what a sight, Jim! Truly, like the old phrase has it, a 'shining sea' . . ."

After a time, he picked up the thread of conversation again. "When the planet began to dry up, and the surface cracked, most of the prehistoric oceans dispersed into the atmosphere. Mars has a low gravitational field, too weak to hang onto water molecules for long, unlike Earth.

"Remember those dustlands, where we met?" he went on. Brant nodded; he remembered them well. "The Argyre," Harbin said. "Once the bottom of an ocean. Well, that narrow, deep chasm across it called the Erebus—one of those cracks in the planetary crust I was talking about. It would seem that not all of the oceanwater dispersed into the atmosphere to be lost forever . . . some, like this, must have leaked into vast caverns beneath the crust, through chasms like the Erebus. No other way to explain it!"

"Yeah, I see what you mean," drawled Brant.

The three Martians had followed them to the hilltop by now, and stood as if struck by lightning, too paralyzed by astonishment to move, even to speak or cry out.

"Chasm or no chasm, when the old ocean seeped down through the crust, it must have picked up a lot of minerals along the way. It must have taken many centuries to happen. Which may explain the curious phenomenon of the luminescence. . . ."

"And maybe even the stone stair!" suggested Brant, surprised at his own sharpness. "There were people living up there on the continent we call Ogygis Regio in those days: I found Zuarra and Suoli in the ruins of one of their cities, remember."

"I recall," Doc said slowly.

"They were sea-kings, maybe. Like the Vikings of old. And they watched their ocean ebb year after year, generation after generation. And cut a stairway down to what remained of their sea. Maybe they venerated it, had religious feelings about it . . . anyway, to hew those thousands of steps out of solid rock would sure require centuries of labor."

Harbin cast him a strange glance. "I'm impressed, my boy. You've a head on your shoulders. I think you have hit on the truth, strange as it sounds to us. But stranger things have happened, and for even less comprehensible reasons . . . the building of the Egyptian pyramids, for example. The Great Wall of China. Built to keep the savage nomads away, but it was the descendants of those very nomads that completed the work, for their ancestors had conquered China by then, wall or no wall."

After a while, they descended the hill to pace the narrow shore. Will Harbin squatted to examine the glittering sand that looked for all the world as if it was carpeted with jewels of every color and description—rubies, pearls, emeralds, topazes, yellow zircons, amethysts, opals, lumps of amber and jade, sapphires, even dull but lucent diamonds.

"Mineral deposits," he decided, "not gems. The water must be incredibly rich in mineral salts. They would coagulate like this, coming together into lumps, forming pebbles by conglomeration, under the movement of the waves."

Zuarra bent to pick one of these from the shore. It was smooth as glass, more oval than teardrop-shaped, and blazing with rich colors, brown, amber, gold, all streaked through with crimson. She exclaimed over the beauty of the thing.

"Keep it, then," shrugged Brant good-humoredly. "Nobody else is likely to stake a claim to it."

She gave him a shy smile, dimpling most charmingly, and tucked it away in a pocket of her robe. Brant was studying the sea. The surface seemed in constant turmoil, swirling this way and that, coiling into miniature shallow whirlpools, but there didn't seem to be much in the way of waves.

He pointed this out to Will Harbin.

"Not this far below the surface, even if the moons of Mars were big enough to make tides like our Moon does back home," murmured the older man. "Chemical ferment, perhaps; amoeboid life. Even centrifugal force, caused by the planet as it swings on its axis."

He bent, dabbling his forefinger in the milky luminance, tasting a drop of the seawater gingerly. Then he made a face.

"Mineral salts, all right!" he exclaimed. "Ugh, what a taste! And so thick with salt it would rust stainless steel. Well, there's the last proof of our theorising . . . to get that rich in minerals, the water just had to seep through interstices in the crust for long centuries."

At Brant's side, Zuarra spoke up timidly:

"Is it . . . is all of this *water*, O Brant?" she whispered.

He nodded. "Water of a sort," he grunted. "But I wouldn't try drinking any of it, if I were you. Which makes me think, Doc—are we likely to find any fresh water down here? We certainly can't drink *this* stuff, and my canteen's nearly empty. I guess all of them are, by now. And we're going to start getting mighty thirsty before long."

"As to springs of fresh water, who can say?" was Harbin's reply. "Maybe, maybe not. But there's lots of juice in those huge mushrooms, so we won't suffer from lack of fluids."

He scratched his nose. "Pity you couldn't carry the pressure-still along. It could easily have been adjusted to extract the pure water from this mineral muck. As it is, we may have to do it by ourselves, by the slow process of evaporation and condensation. Collect the sea-water in some kind of container, boil it over a fire—the dry stalks of some of those fallen fungus-trees back in the forest ought to burn like tinder. Then we rig a shield out of something . . . maybe the nioflex of our thermal-suits, collect the condensation, funnel it off . . ." his voice trailed away, uncertain as to the details.

Brant grinned. "Oh, I guess we can put our heads together and figure out some way of doing it."

He glanced out over the surface of the luminous sea. "Can we take baths in this muck, d'you suppose? It's been so long since I've had a swim, or even a halfway decent bath, it sure would be a treat!"

Doc grinned. "Expect it would be safe enough," he said. "One thing's certain, you won't have to worry about drowning, no matter how much about swimming you may have forgotten. In *that* sea, you couldn't drown if you tried to!"

Brant looked puzzled. Harbin chuckled.

"Water's so rich with salt and minerals, it's hard to sink in. Look—" he picked up one of the larger gemlike pebbles, weighed it in his palm. It looked about as heavy as a baseball, but when he tossed it a little ways out to sea, it *floated*.

"Just like Great Salt Lake in Utah, or the Dead Sea in Palestine," he said. "Our bodies are pretty buoyant as it is. In this stuff, though, we'd float like corks."

Brant shook his head wonderingly.

"This is sure one hellova strange place," he said, with a low whistle of amazement.

"It is that," Doc agreed. And then he added, soberly: "And I've a feeling we've only seen a few of the marvels we're going to discover before long."

And, as usual, the older man proved right, eventually.

Since it had been long enough since Agila had devoured the meat of the giant mushrooms, and he showed no signs of sickness or discomfort, they returned to the midst of the fungus-forest and made a zestful meal, sampling the flesh of different-colored growths.

Brant found them all tasty, but the one he liked best was his own discovery. The huge stalk, crowned with its nodding head the size of a barrel, was silvery-gray on the outside, mottled with irregular lavender spots. Inside, the flesh proved creamy in color and of the consistency of vanilla pudding. But it tasted like nothing else than the finest white meat of the tuna fish. The succulent, meaty taste pleased them all, even the three Martians, who had never tasted anything remotely like fish in their lives.

"Well," sighed Brant contentedly, patting a full stomach at the conclusion of their feast, "after weeks of canned rations and lizard meat, it's good to have a decent meal again!"

Harbin grinned in agreement. "Even if the dishes were a

trifle exotic," he said. "The meat from that tuna-tree might taste even better with a chewier consistency. We could try broiling slices over a slow fire. . . ."

Brant stifled a huge yawn. "Incidentally, Doc . . . d'you suppose it ever gets dark in this place?"

"I doubt it. We've been here quite a while by now, and the luminosity does not seem to wax or wane. We're going to have to learn to sleep with the lights on, that's all."

18
The Lovers

They were all weary from their exertions on the stone stair, and felt emotionally drained from the succession of marvels they had found in this weird underground world, and were not long in seeking their rest.

In this humid warmth, there was no need for bedrolls or blankets. The travelers simply lay down wherever they were and fell asleep almost instantly. The dewy moss was springy and soft, and made as comfortable a bed as any they could recently recall.

During the night—odd word to use in this land of perpetual day, but old habits are difficult to break—Brant woke. His bladder was full and he felt the need to relieve himself. He rose and padded a little ways into the depths of the fungus-forest for privacy, and found that two of his companions had also sought seclusion, but for a somewhat different reason.

Agila and little Suoli lay wrapped in each other's arms, their bodies moving vigorously in the act of love. From her moans and whimpers and soft little sighs, the young woman did not seem exactly unwilling.

Brant stopped short at the sight and lingered for a moment on the edge of the little glade in which the lovers lay. It was none of his business, and the two had every right to their private pleasures, so he withdrew silently. They had not noticed him come and were too busy to notice him leave.

But their passion had another witness, it seemed. Not far

from the place where Brant had stood, discovering them, stood another. It was Zuarra. The expression on her face was unreadable, but it did not look to Brant like either sorrow or anger, nor even jealousy. There was no telling how long she had stood there, watching the two from the concealment of a tall spotted mushroom-tree.

As Brant went past her, she turned and saw him, and reached out to take his arm. Somehow—and afterwards he could never quite remember how it came about—she was in his arms, her firm breasts warm against his bare chest, her mouth sweet and eager under his own.

They exchanged no words, for none were needed. Arm in arm they turned to seek another place, and when they found a cozy bower, sheltered by thickly set mushroom-trees, they sank to the soft cushion of the moss and made love hungrily, almost savagely, coupling like beasts.

When they were done, and he thought to rise, she clung to him, locking her arms around his neck.

"Stay in me," she whispered hoarsely, and he did. After a time, they dozed off, only to wake and to love again. And the second time it was even better. He discovered in her a hungry passion equal to his own, a tirelessness and a vigor. And she found in him a warmth, a tenderness, a gentle strength she had never found in another man. It was, to her, as satisfying, as draining, as the love of women, but different, very different, in a way she could not put into words.

When he awoke at last, it was to discover her sitting tailor-fashion nearby, regarding him with thoughtful eyes. He grinned and she too smiled a soft, contented smile. When he reached out to touch her, to caress her body, she came into his arms and they kissed.

"Has it been a long time for you, O Brant?" she whispered.

It had been a long time since Brant had a woman. He nodded, adding: "And even longer since I've had a woman like you." She smiled demurely.

"It has been long for Zuarra, too," she admitted. "Never has she enjoyed love with any man as much as she enjoys it with you."

They rose to their feet and went back to the clearing where they found Suoli and Agila fast asleep, and Will Harbin grinned at them. He wanted to remark further on the parallels between this lovely place and Eden—something to the effect that it looked as though Adam and Eve had tasted of the apple, but held his peace.

For breakfast they toasted thick slices of the tunafish-tree over a small fire which Brant touched to smoldering with a thin, quick beam from his power gun. It was even more delicious than it had been the "evening" before.

They were going to have to invent new terms for such familiar words as morning, afternoon, night and evening, for these words did not apply to this weird and wonderful world that lay dreaming like Paradise, bathed in a pearly light like that of the morning of the First Day.

After breakfast, Harbin and Brant set about rigging up a crude still in which to boil the impurities out of the seawater. It was not an easy job, for they lacked the proper utensils, but they found at length that their makeshift still worked well enough, although it was a lengthy and boring process, waiting for the steam from the boiling water to condense into enough pure water for them to sate their thirsts.

Brant and Zuarra had few words for each other, but their eyes met frequently and very often they touched, with a pretense of casualness. Agila and Suoli only had eyes for each other and hardly seemed to notice. As for the old scientist, he chattered volubly, if only to fill the silence.

Later that day, Brant caught a dragonfly napping and killed the creature with Agila's knife, which he had not returned to him since their brief fist-fight many days before. Harbin examined the creature with alert curiosity, dissecting it with the knife. The bowie-like blade was unsuited to such delicate work, but Harbin did the best he could. He found that the tubular body contained a sizable quantity of meat, which he toasted over the smoldering coals of their fire.

When the others proved a bit too squeamish to taste the stuff, he sampled it himself. "Tastes quite a bit like escargot," he pronounced, chewing judiciously. "A slice of lemon would help; but it's not bad. Well, now we know that when we get tired of eating from the mushroom-trees, we can vary our diet somewhat.

"Think there's any fish in the ocean, Doc?" asked Brant.

"Doubt it very much. There are none to be found in Great Salt Lake or the Dead Sea, either. And this underground ocean is saltier than both."

That "night" after the travelers dined on more mushroom-meat, and sought their rest, Zuarra and Brant stole away into the forest to make love. It was richer and deeper this third time, the hungry wanting somewhat satisfied. They lacked the urgency they had felt before, and took the time to explore each other's bodies with sensitivity and tenderness.

"How long do we intend to remain in this strange world, O Brant?" Zuarra asked, after the loving, as they lay together with naked limbs entwined.

"Who knows?" he yawned. "Until the outlaws go away, I guess. But it's not a bad place to be. Warm, comfortable, plenty of food. And if there are any predators down here, we've yet to see them."

They kissed, and drowsed into sleep.

And awoke suddenly with lances touching their throats.

It had taken Tuan and his men less time to get down the stony stair than it had taken Brant's party, for they were all lean and rangy men, hard and tough, while Brant had been slowed somewhat by the women, especially little Suoli.

But they had come at last. And Brant wondered if they had already captured the others, and cursed himself silently for having left his power guns behind with his clothing. But who could have thought that he might need his guns in this peaceful garden?

I should have thought, he said grimly to himself. After all, he had known there was a very good chance the outlaws might follow them down the stair. He inwardly cursed himself for letting the beauty of this place and the marvels within it, and the woman who lay at his side, lull him away from his usual wariness. Well, there was never any good crying over spilt milk—or blood, either.

A booted foot kicked him in the side. He gave voice to an involuntary grunt and would have sprung to his feet, but for the long lance level with his breast.

One of the outlaws, a villanous-looking rogue with cold, mean eyes as unblinking as those of a cobra, grinned, revealing broken and discolored teeth, and pressed with the lance a little.

The point just broke his skin. Brant felt a drop of blood trickle down his bare chest.

He exchanged a long look with Zuarra. Her face was expressionless and there was no fear in her eyes as she looked at him. But they were lying so close together that he could feel how rapidly her heart was beating beneath her proud breasts.

Yes, the Serpent was in Eden, at last. . . .

"Let them rise to their feet," ordered Tuan, "and lead them back to where the other dogs are penned. Bind their wrists behind their backs." He stalked away toward the place where, presumably, Harbin and the others were held prisoner.

Brant watched with a heavy heart as the men bound Zuarra. Oddly, they did not insult her body with their hands. Instead, they looked her naked body over from face to feet with cool, appraising eyes. They wore not the expression of men whose minds were lingering on thoughts of rape. Instead, they examined her with their eyes as if looking over something that could be sold for a good price.

19

The Flying Man

Looking weary, Will Harbin lay on the moss with two warriors standing over him.

Whimpering and blubbering, Suoli, similarly bound, cowered at the feet of another warrior, while Agila sprawled naked, eyes wide with fear, a little beyond where his woman was huddled.

They had all been taken unawares. And Brant silently damned himself for not having taken the proper precautions which would have prevented this debacle. He was too old a Mars hand to be caught like this, quite literally, napping.

When the five captives had all been bound, Tuan surveyed them one by one, with hard, measuring eyes. He was a tall rascal, his kilt unmarked by the colors of his nation, which, of course, showed that he was *aoudh*—an outcast. But the blood of princes flowed in his veins, and you could see it in his stance, in the ramrod-straightness wherewith he held himself, and in something of the poise of his head.

He strolled over to where Agila crouched, licking lips dry with fear, and nudged the naked man in the ribs with the toe of his boot.

"Dog, it was you who stole from me the sacred dish of my ancestors," he hissed between thin lips. "Not only did you commit the crime of theft from one who had shown you the hospitality of his camp, but you fled from justice like a coward in the dark."

Agila lowered his eyes to the ground, his lean, bony face surly and his eyes sullen. But he again licked his dry lips.

Tuan eyed the man contemptuously, then kicked him in the ribs. Agila cried out, and fell on his side.

"For your ending," purred Tuan, "we shall devise something interesting and novel. Perhaps we shall be able to outdo Kohharin himself," he added, in reference to an ancient and legendary king mentioned in The Book, whose name had become renowned for the ingenuity of the torments which he had of old inflicted upon his enemies.

Then Tuan turned to survey the two naked women. "Of you, I know nothing, and will be charitable," he said. "Your bodies will be sold in Ahour, perhaps to a pleasure-house, and it shall be your fate to open your thighs to men that are not of your choosing!"

Brant growled and bristled at those words. Tuan turned his head and looked at him, and at Harbin.

"As for you, *f'yagha*, you have befouled the treasure of my princely ancestors with your eyes and your outworlder touch. As well, you abetted this dog in his flight, and aided him with your wits, your guns, and your water. His fate shall be your fate, while the world lasts!"

Then he strode away to confer with one or two of the other men of his band, leaving his prisoners alone with their thoughts. And bitter, lonely thoughts they were. . . .

The outlaw chieftain inspected their garments and gear idly, finding little that pleased him save their guns. Energy weapons were prized possessions among the People, as Brant knew very well. After all, in leaner times, he had run guns to the native princelings, himself.

The "morning" wore on. Under close guard, the captives were left bound and helpless. Brant surreptitiously tested his bonds, but they were too tough, and too cunningly tied, for even his burly strength to loosen, much less to snap.

He watched Tuan carefully. Even though the chieftain had been the keeper of the pale gold dish with its engraved ancient map, he was obviously as puzzled and impressed at discovering this subterranean cavern world as had been the members of Brant's party. Obviously, to him the dish had simply been a precious relic of the past, an heirloom, a family treasure, nothing more.

He measured Tuan's warriors with thoughtful eyes. They were a lean and hungry band of ruffians, men without a clan, hardened by the lifelong struggle to survive in the hostile wilderness of desert Mars, and probably accustomed to every crime he could think of, and a few more that he couldn't.

They were hard riders, excellent trackers, and, as he knew from the brief battle at the mouth of the cave, dangerous and veteran warriors. They were also heavily armed. About half of the fourteen were armed with laser rifles, the others with power guns, and all of them had knives—the long-bladed, heavy, deadly Martian knives they called *s'zouks*. As efficient and dangerous a weapon, in skilled and practiced hands, as had been the bowie knives on the American frontier.

And he had no doubt that all of these desert wolves were well practiced in using them. . . .

Even if he had been able to get his hands loose, they were too wary to be taken by surprise, and there were too many of them for him to hope to fight, with even the slightest chances of success.

He also noticed—with bitter amusement—that their bristling store of weaponry had newly been augmented by the twin laser rifles which Doc Harbin and his native scout had held when Brant and the women first encountered them, as well as Brant's own pair of power pistols, and even the long knife Agila had carried in his boot.

What was needed here—he thought wryly—was some sort of a diversion to distract the outlaws just long enough for the five prisoners to struggle to their feet (for the outlaws had not bound their captives' ankles, for some reason, perhaps being short of ropes). Then, with any luck, they could all hightail it into the depths of the fungus-forest, and, with a little more luck, find places to hide in whatever sort of terrain might lie on the far side of the grove.

Once safe, at least relatively, they could in time chew through each other's bonds and be off. Although off to *where*, Brant had no idea. *A diversion*. . . .

Brant uttered a mirthless chuckle. Well, the sudden appearance of a hungry dinosaur about the height of a two-story building would be adequate! A charging herd of woolly mammoths would come in handy. Brant would even have settled for a hunting-pack of sabertooth tigers, if any were available.

He rather doubted that they were, though. He had yet to see any wildlife bigger than a couple of outsized dragonflies, and these seemed harmless enough.

He leaned back as comfortably as he could, and closed his eyes, resting himself and conserving his strength for whatever opportunity to make a break for it might, but probably would not, occur.

When he opened his eyes again it was because the sea breeze had wafted to his nostrils the scent of burning fungus-stalks. Tuan and his band had started a bonfire, touching off the dry, fibrous stuff even as Brant had earlier, with a touch of needle-beam. The stuff burned like tinder.

Brant narrowed his eyes. The desert warriors were rigging a makeshift spit over the fire, using their metal spears. As they did so, they grinned and chuckled among themselves, for all the world like a passel of Apaches about to scalp a few White Eyes. They glanced occasionally at their captives, and the expression in their eyes was cruel and gloating.

Brant shot a glance at Agila. The lean rogue was wide-eyed and panting in fear, and Brant didn't blame him.

The outlaws obviously intended to roast the poor bastard over a slow fire, Brant grimly guessed. And his stomach-muscles knotted in sympathy.

For he and Will Harbin would probably be second course, once Agila had died screaming, burned to a crisp, as the saying goes. The women would be sold into slavery in the slave markets of the nearest city of the People, once the chieftain had led his band back up the stony stair to the surface.

Time was running out, although it would take Agila hours to die, if Tuan and his warriors did the job properly, and in those interminable, grisly hours before it was his and Doc's turn for the torture, anything at all might happen.

Brant rather wished he had been a religious man, for if so, he could have prayed right then and there, without cowardly hypocrisy. Because if anybody ever needed a miracle to happen, it was him and his companions. . . .

Jesting obscenely among themselves, the outlaws strolled over to where Agila crouched in terror, and lifted him to his feet, and began to truss him to one of the spear-shafts. These lances were of metal, of course, not wood, for wood is virtually unknown on the Desert World. The heat of the metal shaft along his back, shoulders and buttocks would add a certain extra something to Agila's agony, once they began to turn him slowly over on the makeshift spit over the roaring fire.

Brant looked at his companions. Suoli lay huddled face-down in the moss, blubbering hysterically, her entire body shaking convulsively as she sobbed and shuddered.

Will Harbin's face was grave but composed, and the older man's eyes were closed and his lips moved slightly in prayer, perhaps.

Then he looked at Zuarra, seated beside him on the moss with her ankles crossed tailor-fashion. She held herself proudly, her spine as straight as an arrow. Her eyes were stony, her lips tight, her expression aloof.

God, she was a brave woman, Brant thought. He had never known a braver!

She turned to meet his gaze, her eyes calm and level and unfaltering. Their eyes locked.

And in that moment he realized that he loved her, and she read it in his face and smiled.

20
The Flying Boy

The outlaws lifted the spear to which Agila was securely bound onto the supports they had rigged over the bonfire for their makeshift spit. As the heat smote him—face, breast, belly and thighs—he squeezed his eyes shut and clamped his lips together tightly, screwing up his face, and letting no sound escape him.

Tuan watched appraisingly, a slight smile playing about his lips.

"O, brave and braver still is the skulking thief in the night!" he exclaimed tauntingly. "But the courageous silence of the dog Agila will not last very long . . . soon will he writhe and wriggle on the spit. And then a whimper or a gasp will come . . . and then, mayhap, some weeping or crying out. It will perhaps be half a *kua*, mayhap a trifle less, before the screaming will commence. And it will be happy music to the ears of Tuan!"

Half a *kua* was a measurement of Martian time the equivalent to about ten minutes, Brant knew. He rather agreed with Tuan's estimate of how long Agila could hold his tongue.

And then it happened.

Tuan glanced up suddenly, in the direction of the hills, and his eyes widened in amazement and disbelief. He uttered a harsh croak, an involuntary cry.

Behind Brant, Will Harbin cried out, "Good God!" in a shaky voice.

And Brant himself looked up.

There came hurtling through the air toward their camp, heading inland from the sea, a Flying Boy.

He was lithe and naked, pale golden, hairless. And he bore in one fist a long, glittering lance.

At first glimpse, it seemed to them all that he was winged. But then, as he flashed down upon them, scattering the outlaws into howling flight, they saw that he was mounted between the flickering, thrumming wings of a gigantic dragonfly.

It was obviously akin to the flying things they had seen in the fungus-forest, one of which Brant had slain with the knife, and Doc had cooked and sampled its meat.

But that one was only as long as Brant's arm. *This* fantastic creature was the length of a six-man canoe, and its glittering wings of sheeted opal must have a forty-foot spread.

As his amazing steed flashed by overhead, the golden youth leaned from the saddle—for now Brant had a closer look, he observed that he was strapped into a high saddle woven, it seemed, of wicker. With the flat head of his lance, he caught Agila in the ribs, with a blow just strong enough to push the whole spit-contraption over into the moss beyond the fire.

Agila flopped, wriggled, gasping, rubbing his blistered parts against the cool, damp moss.

Brant got clumsily to his feet, and stood staring skywards. The aerial knight soared by overhead, banked in a sharp turn, and came about for another pass at them. He bent over to peer at them, and Brant noticed only that his eyes were glinting amber, and that he was quite young, long-legged, smoothly built, and so strikingly handsome as almost to be worthy of being called beautiful, although in a boyish way.

Brant nudged Zuarra with his foot.

"*Up* girl! Run for it. Doc! Suoli—stop your blubbering! On your feet, all of you—make for the grove!"

Zuarra and Will Harbin, at least, instantly understood Brant's notion. While the outlaw band scattered in witless terror, like jackrabbits startled by a hunting hawk, they could lose themselves in the forest.

With Zuarra loping along at his side, Brant broke into a

clumsy staggering run for the edge of the clearing. Then, several things happened so quickly, that ever after it was tough for him to sort them out in sequence.

Suddenly, to his dazed eyes, the sky was filled with naked golden children mounted on enormous dragonflies. There must have been a couple of dozen of them, perhaps twice that number. Uttering shrill, exuberant cries and brandishing their glittering lances, they wheeled in tight formation over the clearing.

Then Will Harbin cried out for help. A coil of braided rope settled about his shoulders, bringing him to a halt; another caught him about the hips. Yelling and kicking, he was dragged off his feet and into the air.

As Brant paused uncertainly on the edge of the clearing, looking back, one of the aerial riders spotted him, gave voice to a shrill halloo, and headed for him quicker than the eye could follow. Brant did not even have time to blink before he, too, was lassoed and hauled into the air.

Zuarra screamed once as her kicking heels left the moss and she was born aloft.

Then, the speed of their flight making their eyes blur with tears, they were carried off on swift, thrumming wings toward the luminous sea.

Brant looked back, squinting his watering eyes against the wind. Zuarra, Harbin, Suoli, Tuan, and all of the outlaws had been captured by the flying boys. All kicked and squirmed and seemed unharmed. He discovered later that one of the flying youths, the first to have discovered them, had returned to rescue Agila from his bondage.

Looking up, he realized that each of the dragonfly-riders was sharing their weight. That is, he had been lassoed almost simultaneously by two of the nude children. It would seem, then, that the dragonflies, no matter how enormous, had to share the weight of captives between them.

The aerial creatures had two sets of wings at either side, sprouting from the same boulderlike bunch of muscles. For all their strength, however, they had to share the extra burden of a captive.

They were gorgeous, the super-dragonflies. Even in this precarious position, he could appreciate their rich coloring. Their long, stiff, tube-shaped bodies varied from the hue of burnished bronze to metallic green like verdigris, and sparkled in the light of the radiant sea beneath them. The droning of their wings in flight was sonorous, and their eye-bunches glistened like clustered wet black gems.

He noticed that the strange glassy lances borne by the pilots were employed in lieu of bit or bridle, for the giant dragonflies wore no reins. Instead, they were guided by these long, flat-bladed spears. It seemed the flying creatures had sensitive nodules on the top of their heads: a tap or a rap on certain of these communicated the commands of their riders. Up, down, right, left, went the message of the tappings.

He had, of course, thought of them as weapons. It seemed, however, that they were not.

As for the riders themselves, all of those who were within the range of his vision were uniformly young. This would seem to make good sense: for all their size, the super-dragonflies had little in the way of lifting-power. The riders most suited to the craft were young boys between the ages of twelve and fourteen, as he later learned.

They flew out over the phosphorescent ocean, the captors and their captives, and descended before very long to an astonishing vessel. It was like unto no ship that Brant had ever seen or heard of. Its shape was that of a crescent, with a high forecastle and an equally tall aft-structure. And it seemed to possess neither sails nor oarbanks.

Even stranger, it was not made out of wood, but woven out of something like bundles of reeds or wicker.

The flyers hovered above the deck midships and—dropped their captive quarry!

They landed upon a springy deck woven, it seemed, of rattan, which gave beneath their weight. All of them were bound and helpless, the party led by Brant with bound wrists, the outlaws tangled in those braided lassoes.

The rattan decks gave beneath their weight. In no time, other excited mariners, young and naked and golden, took

them into custody. Whereupon, the mounted dragonflies settled into the mastlike superstructure above the ship.

Brant had noticed these branching masts devoid of sails or
cordage, with naught but rope-ladders, but had been too busy
to think much about them, so swiftly did the movement of
events go forward. Now he saw that the many-branched
masts were the roosting-places of the super-dragonflies.

Their mounts tethered to these aerial perches, the naked
pilots swarmed with agility down the rope ladders, to engage
the other mariners in a babble of excited jabbering. Brant
caught Doc Harbin's eye and called across to him.

"Can you understand any of their talk, Doc?"

Harbin shook his head. "The most ancient form of the
Tongue, surely. I can read some of it, in the written form, but
. . . I can catch the meaning of about one word in six, at
best."

"They don't seem as much hostile as excited," Brant
remarked.

"Any why not?" demanded the old scientist. "After all,
we're probably the first strangers they've encountered in
a few million years!"

Which gave Brant pause to think.

Were they going to end up in a slaughterhouse, a zoo, a
prison, or a private menagerie of oddities and curiosities?

Time would tell . . . as it usually does.

V

SEA-KINGS
OF MARS

21

The Voyage

With strangely shaped knives, the golden children cut their bonds and also removed the lassoes. They gathered closely about their captives, chattering excitedly among themselves, reaching out to touch with curious fingers their hair, and the Martian furcaps.

Brant looked them over alertly. They were all young, and many of them were no more than boys—including the one who had lassoed him. This lad looked to be about twelve, maybe thirteen. He had long, coltish legs, finely muscled arms and shoulders, and bright golden eyes with a glint of mischief in them. Later, Brant learned the boy's name was Kirin.

Not only were they bald but completely devoid of any body hair at all, he noted. This made a lot of sense to Brant, for the humidity and warmth of this climate caused his scalp to perspire most annoyingly, and the rivulets of sweat had been trickling down into his eyes. Baldness would be a survival-trait down here, he thought to himself.

The boys were all completely naked, save for light, glittering harnesses made of some material he could not at once identify, but certainly not leather. These consisted of two straps over the shoulders, buckled to a strap which encircled the body just below the nipples, and a further strap about the hips.

The harnesses were fashioned of some scaly, glinting stuff colored rich bronze or peacock blue or red-gold. They seemed to be partly utilitarian and partly ornamental. That is, buckles and hooks hung from them, and attached to these the nude youths wore certain tools or implements. Otherwise, the straps served mainly to support gemmed pins, badges of precious metals, and such ornaments.

The knives wherewith they had cut the bonds from the two Earthsiders and the women, seemed ill-suited to such a task. They didn't look at all to Brant like weapons, more like kitchen utensils.

They were made, he noticed, of transparent metal, clear as crystal. And the long slender lances the aerial riders had carried were fashioned from the same material. Brant had never seen such a curious metal in all his years on Mars. He filed it away mentally as just one more mystery. Later on, in Zhah, he discovered that the golden race extracted the glassy metal from the waters of the shining sea by a process akin to electrolytic baths. This made sense: after all, the seawater was heavy with mineral salts of every kind.

The flying youths had captured all of them, including the outlaws, and had rescued Agila, who crouched whimpering on the springy rattan deck, while Suoli crooned and fluttered over him, soothing his hurts with kisses.

Most of the outlaws were still armed, although only with knives and pistols, for they had dropped their laser rifles and spears when lassoed by the flyers. Tuan, at that moment, was fingering the butt of one of Brant's own power guns, glancing around with hard, calculating eyes.

Brant caught his eye. "I wouldn't try it, Tuan," he said in low tones, cocking a thumb skywards. The chieftain looked up to see the monster dragonflies on their curious perches. Many were watching the scene below with inscrutable eyes of glittering ocelli.

Tuan flinched a little, and nodded curtly to the Earthsider as if agreeing.

Since they did not seem to be under any sort of constraint and were merely surrounded by a jabbering mob of naked boys, Brant ambled over to where Tuan stood and spoke to him.

"I don't know but what those flying monsters might not

come to the aid of their riders, if provoked," he said. "Lay off the guns."

Tuan raked them with a glance of contempt. "They are but boys," he grunted harshly. "Soft, effeminate—weaklings, by the look of them."

"Yeah, and they're also completely unarmed," drawled Brant cooly. "Is it Honor for a warrior chieftain to fire upon naked, unarmed children?"

The shaft went home, as Brant had known it would. Honor to the People was more than life or wealth—an indefinable, precious quality to be nurtured, not depleted. Even outlaws such as Tuan were sensitive when it came to matters of that nature. He flinched at Brant's carefully chosen words, and gave him a hard look from ugly eyes.

"There is still blood to be paid between Tuan and you," the chieftain reminded him.

"I know," Brant nodded. "But let's settle the private feud once we're out of this mess. Otherwise, it might cost you the lives of all of your men. We have no way of knowing what resources, what defenses, what peculiar powers, these strange people might possess."

That went home, too. As superstitious as all wandering nomads, Tuan had been stuffed full of tales of ghosts, gods and goblins—well, the Martian equivalents, at least—from his mother's knee.

"It shall be as you say, *f'yagh*," he grunted sourly.

"I have a name," Brant reminded him. "It is Brant."

"Brant, then!" snarled the other. The Earthsider gave him a cool smile and strolled back to Zuarra's side.

While Brant had been in brief conversation with the outlaw chieftain, Will Harbin had been trying to converse with the golden youths. They were mystified by his words, whose meaning eluded their comprehension, although he spoke to them in the oldest form of the Tongue with which he had any facility, and strove to modify his pronunciation to their own.

Eventually they were led into the spacious forecastle, where soft cushions of gaudy colors were strewn in cozy profusion. Strange food and drink was served to them in ceramic bowls and goblets, and the sources of only a few of them could the travelers identify as being similar to some of the mushroom-meat they had sampled back in the fungus-forest.

There was a golden, sweet wine, like honey-hearted mead, and a rich red brandy that savored of apples, somehow, and a light sparkling wine, like vintage champagne, but lime-green. Brant had tasted something like these from various of the mushroom-trees. In particular, he guessed the golden mead was derived from the dripping honeycomb-stuff they had eaten first.

Tuan cautiously sampled the strong red brandy, coughed at its unexpected bite, and pronounced it a fair enough beverage, on the whole. Then he lifted his cup to the smiling boy with the jug, asking for a refill.

While some of the food and drink was familiar, many others were not. There was a savory stew in which small nuggets of chewy meat of beeflike consistency swam in a highly spiced red sauce, for one. And another was a ragout of stringy meat-fibers soaking in a thick, creamy gravy.

Everything was so completely delicious, that the travelers merely shrugged off the question of where the food came from, and wolfed it down.

Sometime while they were at the feast, the odd vessel got underway. Brant had wondered earlier how a ship with neither sails nor oars could be made to travel, but the answer, when it came, was simplicity itself.

They were towed by the dragonflies!

Tethered by long lines to their perches in the complicated mastlike structures overhead, the point and flank creatures bearing mounted riders to guide them in the desired direction, the winged creatures drew the lightweight but stoutly built craft over the glowing waters with apparent ease.

Brant and the others stared at this strange sight with wondering eyes. The luminous sea, the naked laughing children on their fantastic flying steeds, the elfin vessel itself—it was all like some scene from a fairy tale, or an illustration in an old children's book, Brant thought.

What Zuarra, or Suoli, or the other natives thought was beyond conjecture. Perhaps they were beyond amazement itself, by this time, their imaginations stunned by the sheer profusion of marvels they had encountered on this weird journey below the planet's ancient crust.

The boy who had captured Brant, an eager, bright-eyed little imp, had attached himself to the tall man with a sort of proprietary interest. Seeing that neither could understand each other, the boy laid his hand on his breast and said, carefully, "Kirin!"

Brant nodded, repeating the name a time or two until he had the pronunciation right. Then the lad laid his hand on Brant's chest with an inquiring look.

"Brant," the man said, grinning.

"Pran-dt?" murmured the boy. The man shook his head, and kept repeating his name until the lad, Kirin, had it right. Then they began a language-lesson, Brant pointing to various parts of the body, to the sea, to the boat, and so on, and trying to memorize the words that Kirin gave him.

Got to learn the language somehow, thought Brant to himself. *We might be here a lot longer than we think.*

Will Harbin, in the meantime, was getting language-lessons of his own. His tutor, surprisingly, was a young girl!

They had not realized at once that not all of the slim, golden children were male. Harbin's teacher, Aulli, was of about the same age as young Kirin, and every bit as long-legged, flat-chested as the boy, her breasts not even having begun to bud. Lacking noticeable breasts, the girls mingled with the boys in one naked, bald, golden mob, to the eyes of the newcomers.

Tuan listened suspiciously for a time to the exchange of nouns and verbs—but they were on to simple verbs by that point, "jump," "sit," "run," and the like. Then he snorted and stalked away to join his men. He had gathered them into a tight group amidship and they kept much to themselves.

It did not occur to Brant to wonder exactly where the ship was heading, until somewhat later. Even if he had thought about it at the time, he could never have guessed.

22

The Monster

When they became hungry or thirsty, the golden children ate or drank, careless of whether their fellows were hungry or not. There seemed to be no particular discipline or regularity about the faery ship that Brant could see.

And when they became sleepy, they simply lay down carelessly wherever they were, and curled up for a nap.

"These kids obviously don't have any enemies to worry about," Brant observed to Harbin. "If they did, they wouldn't be so lax about regulating the things they do. It's a wonder they ever get anything done."

"I've been wondering why they were flying over the mainland, myself," mused the scientist. "Maybe just for a boyish romp. . . ."

Brant called his friend's attention to two youngsters who were casually making love a little ways apart from where the two men sat.

"Wonder how they keep the birth rate down," chuckled Brant. Then, as the two lovers reversed position, he reddened and looked hastily away. For they were both boys of about fourteen or so.

"Maybe that's how!" chuckled Doc.

They ceased puzzling over the motive for the flight of aerial riders who had captured them a bit later on, when a similar flight of whooping boys and girls took off from the perches, and headed out to sea, waving their glassy lances and calling to each other. They returned to the ship an hour later, their lassoes heavy with fat, glistening creatures that flopped and wriggled.

"Sea-slugs," Harbin decided. "Floating on the surface in schools or whatever the proper term would be, perhaps feeding on algae. The sea has some life, after all!"

Brant grunted a heavy monosyllable, chewing on his underlip and wondering queasily to himself if *that* had been the source of the lumps of meat in the peppery sauce of which they had eaten earlier. He put the question firmly out of his mind, deciding he would rather *not* know.

They watched as the laughing children sliced up the greasy, glistening sluglike creatures, prying out the more succulent inner meat, which they popped into bubbling kettles swung from the rafters of the galley. The superstructure of the ship, by the way, was quite open. There were no walls, just posts and braces, covered with rattan screens you could easily see right through.

Doc ambled over to investigate the cooking pots, and returned with a baffled frown on his face. "Boiling hot water, with herbs and spices in it," he announced.

"So," yawned Brant, who was getting sleepy.

"There's no sign of a fire," Harbin said. "Be hard enough, even dangerous, to maintain any kind of a fire or oven on a ship as flimsy, and as flammable, as this one is. One strong wave, and the deck would be afire in dozens of places, just from the scattering coals!"

Brant suggested they put the problem down as one more of the many mysteries of this fantastic cavern-world, and rolled over to go to sleep for a while.

Brant awoke a time later when a large hand was laid upon his naked shoulder, then removed. He sat up on one elbow to find Tuan squatting on his heels nearby, looking at him gravely.

"Well, what is it that the chieftain Tuan wishes of Brant?" he asked, using the more polite and formal mode of the Tongue.

"Tuan has conferred with his warriors," said the other gruffly. "All of us are being borne away into slavery; there is no other answer to the question of why the Strange Ones captured us and are carrying us away.''

"Brant doubts the truth of that supposition, but continue.''

"The children are without weapons—even the strange spears they bear are used only for the control of their riding-beasts,'' observed the chieftain. Brant nodded: he had examined one of the lances, finding the flat, leaf-shaped blade dull, with neither edge nor point that was sharp enough to do injury.

"Say on.''

"It is true, even as Brant has spoken, that to fire upon the children would cause a warrior to lose Honor,'' muttered Tuan. "But we are all stronger than they are, being grown men and women, and can overpower them with ease, merely binding them. Then we can return to the place of the stair . . .''

"How does Tuan plan to run the ship?'' countered Brant. "Do the warriors of Tuan's band, stalwart and brave men all, as Brant has no doubt, think to ride the flying-beasts?''

Tuan opened his mouth, then blinked once or twice, eyes dulling. Obviously, he had not thought of that.

"And is Tuan certain of the direction in which the ship must travel, for us to return to the place of the stair?'' continued Brant. He knew very well that the People had a mysterious, inborn sense of direction that was often uncanny to Earthsiders, but he doubted if the instinct would work very well down here.

"We . . . ah . . . need only go back in the opposite direction,'' said Tuan, but he sounded uncertain.

"It seems to Brant that we may have changed direction slightly, or more than slightly, when we slept or feasted or conversed, ceasing to notice such things.''

"What, then, does Brant suggest? Does he wish to become the slave of careless children, and he a grown man, even a warrior of sorts?''

"It is the suggestion of Brant that there be truce between us, the warriors of Tuan and those who accompanied Brant hither, for the time being. Once we have arrived at our destination, whatever it is, there will be time enough to take such actions as seem best to us all. Remember,'' he added, falling out of the formal mode of speech and into the vernacular, "the children have not disarmed your warriors, O Tuan. I doubt if they even realize the guns are weapons. So we will get to where we're going with our arms intact and ready."

Squatting there, humming a tuneless song under his breath, Tuan chewed it over, finally nodding.

Rising to his feet, he said, "It shall be as Brant advises. A truce—for now."

"And remember one thing I mentioned earlier," Brant said. "We don't know what strange powers these people may have—"

With a nod of acquiescence, Tuan stalked off to rejoin his band.

And Brant went back to sleep.

He was awakened suddenly by a shrill chorus of cries of alarm and consternation. Spring to his feet, he stared around him so as to discover the cause of the commotion. It took him only moments to spot the thing that had alarmed the children.

For, rising out of the luminous sea was something resembling the sea-slugs the flying hunters had captured for their larder. The main difference was the matter of *size*. While the hunters' prey had been no bigger than small dogs, this sea-slug—if that is what it actually was—must have been the great-granddaddy of them all, for it was as big around as a house, and must have been three hundred feet long.

Like the smaller versions they had seen earlier, its jelly-like flesh was lucent to the point of transparency. As it broke the waves again, heaving its glistening, glassy bulk high, he saw that it was blind and faceless, save for a wet, working sphincter-like orifice which must have served it as mouth.

It looked harmless enough, for all its appalling size. But the sheer tonnage of the sea-monster could easily swamp or crush their flimsy vessel.

Will Harbin and the others joined him at the rail, staring with wide eyes at the huge sea-thing, while the golden children squealed and milled in confusion.

Tuan and his warriors came to the rail, hefting their power guns determinedly. Brant grabbed the chieftain's arm.

"Don't fire unless the monster heads in our direction," he

said in urgent tones. "These people have not yet recognized what we carry as being weapons. Why let them find out so soon?"

Tuan nodded grimly, muttering a curt order to his outlaws.

But, as things turned out, the energy weapons were not needed, although suddenly the monstrous sea-slug turned and came for the ship.

Some of the older youths had gone down into the cabins, and now came pelting up the stair holding strange objects in their right hands. These looked for all the world like glass doorknobs, with a rod small enough to hold in the palm of your hand and pointed knobs at either end.

These peculiar implements were carved from some dark, cloudy semilucent mineral that rather resembled lead-crystal, except that within the pointed knobs an eerie spark of blue flame flickered.

The youths pointed the crystal rods at the sea-beast as it came wallowing through the sluggish waves toward the ship.

Brant uttered an exclamation. Zuarra clutched his arm. Harbin stared wildly.

Darts of blue fire shot from the points of the crystal weapons, to stab and burn the jellied flesh of the sea-monster! Its sphincter-like maw opened and shut as if gasping in pain. It writhed, shrinking from the needle-thin bolts of uncanny blue fire. Then it turned away, sinking beneath the surface, and did not reappear.

The travelers looked at one another, wordless.

The youths watched vigilantly for a time, but when the giant slug failed to emerge a second time, they went below to the storage-space to return the strange weapons to their place.

Shaken, Tuan looked at Brant with something like a touch of admiration in his eyes.

"Wise were the counsels of Brant, when he gave warning to Tuan against using our weapons against the children, saying that we knew not what powers they might possess," he said unsteadily.

Brant nodded. So, the ship-people had energy weapons of their own! That was something to think about. . . .

23

The City on the Sea

The next "day" the ship arrived at its destination, and Mars had yet another marvel to reveal.

It was a town of huts large enough to be called a city, and the buildings, which were mostly one-story structures, with a few that reached to two or three stories, were woven, like the ship, out of stiff fibers like wicker or rattan fastened to frames of thicker girth.

But that was not what made the place a marvel.

It was *floating* on the surface of the luminous sea!

The structures of the city were built on rafts, some of these being so small as only to be able to accommodate one hut, while others seemed nearly as big as city blocks back Earthside.

The rafts of all sizes were linked together by rope-bridges suspended from posts, or by ladders and catwalks, and the rafts were held together in the floating colony by thick braided cables and lines.

On Earth such a maritime metropolis could hardly have held together for long, but would have been broken up by the action of wind and wave, storm and tide. Here in this weird world of eternal morning, of course, there were no waves to speak of and the weather seemed perpetually calm, for the travelers had as yet seen no storms. Later they would discover that a gentle rain did fall from time to time, and that the Sea People—as they came to think of the golden subterraneans —collected this precipitation in rooftop troughs to serve as water for drinking, bathing and cooking. Will Harbin could understand the rains easily enough: humidity from the atmosphere collected like dew on the cavern roof and eventually the drops were large enough to make a decent, if mild, little shower.

The floating city was a gorgeous vision as they approached it across the luminous sea. Some of the wicker structures were painted in gay and gaudy profusion of colors that ranged from rose-pink to carnation and vermilion, pale blue, rich greens, indigo, lavender, tangerine—a dazzling variety of colors that made the incredible place look like an elfin city in a fairy tale.

Flags and banners and pennons fluttered from rooftops and gateposts and masts. Gorgeous silken carpets or tapestries hung from every aperture. None of the buildings seemed to have anything like windows, but it seemed that the rattan wall-screens could be fastened and rolled up by an arrangement of ropes and pulleys at wish.

An insubstantial town of Faerie, floating like a mirage on an unknown sea beneath the world. . . .

Their ship moored at the end of a long quay and the travelers and their captors trooped ashore. Here in a sort of harbor, many similar vessels were tethered. Some of these were ships as large as the one that had captured the travelers, while others ranged from the size of canoes and gondolas, down to little dinghys and miniature rafts.

A laughing, cheerful crowd gathered on the dock to greet their returning friends. And here, for the first time, Brant and the others saw the adults of the golden race, discovering the fully-grown of the Sea People to be as naked and hairless as the children had been. The men looked rather soft and languid and effeminate to Brant's way of thinking, and the women tended to be placid and timid, much like Suoli.

It was obvious that the lack of enemies or hostile weather had made the Sea People degenerate over the hundreds of generations since their forefathers had come to the underground world.

The youths were unlading their ship, bringing "ashore" the food they had caught in ceramic jugs. Everyone milled about in happy confusion, staring curiously at Brant and his companions, laughing gaily and chattering among themselves. Many embraced and kissed the mariners as they came ashore, and Brant could not help noticing that, as often as not, youths were kissed by men or other youths, and girls by girls or women. He doubted, from the lascivious nature of this embracing and caressing, that many of these couples were family.

The travelers did not seem to be under any sort of constraint, although bright-eyed young Kirin stuck close to Brant's side throughout the unloading of the ship, and Will Harbin's demure little tutor, Aulli, clung close to the scientist. Brant noticed that she was holding the older man by the hand, and he grinned. A time or two during the voyage he had teased Harbin about his "little girl-friend," at which the old man had sniffed contemptuously, not deigning to honor the remark with reply or denial.

Soon they were led across catwalks and rope-bridges, walking casually right through houses where whole families were busied at domestic tasks. These merely smiled or waved, seemingly undisturbed by their intrusion. *Guess you get used to having no privacy, where anybody can see through the very walls and nobody wears any clothes,* Brant thought.

"What is this place?" he asked young Kirin, who clung gamely to his side through the crush and press of naked bodies.

"It is Zhah," Kirin answered simply. He looked faintly surprised that Brant did not know; but, then, the very concept of *strangers* was a complete novelty to the boy.

"Who is your ruler?"

"Prince Azuri, of the High-Born," said the boy. "And before him it was Princess Suah, also of the High-Born."

"And who are the High-Born, exactly?" he asked curiously. The boy explained, although he had to fumble a bit to find the proper words, that the High-Born were the noblest of the Seven Clans into which the Sea People were divided. When Brant inquired how many rulers the present dynasty had given to Zhah, Kirin looked baffled, as if the question had no meaning to him.

Later on, they deduced that family relationships were so casual among the Sea People as to be irrelevant. The golden people simply took lovers for a time, before drifting away into another love relationship, and if children were begotten, it was hard to tell to which father. It was difficult for Brant and Harbin to see how any sort of distinct clan-grouping could exist here, where the people seldom if ever knew for certain who their fathers were.

"Maybe they count descent through their mothers, and their mothers' mothers, and so on back," suggested Brant to his companion. Harbin shrugged.

"Hard to imagine a matriarchal society such as the one you suggest being ruled over by a prince," the older man said. "I'll ask Aulli how they work it, when I get a chance."

When they were led before him, Prince Azuri proved to be a slender, girlishly pretty youth of sixteen or so. He wore nothing in the way of regalia that would denote his rank, except that, instead of the partly utilitarian and partly ornamental harness worn by everybody else except for very young children, he wore only gems. These were in the form of necklaces, pectorals, rings on both fingers and toes, anklets, armlets, girdles and bracelets. Among the gems were some with which Brant was already familiar from his years of exploration on the surface, including the ho-katha, or fire-stones, and the rare ziriol, the priceless Martian purple rubies.

Cupidity gleamed in the eyes of Tuan and his outlaws. They had also recognized the gems, and wore greedy expressions.

As, by the way, did Agila. . . .

Rather than being presented to the ruler of the Sea People in some ceremonial manner, it was more like being casually introduced to somebody who might be interested in meeting you.

And the Prince was very interested, indeed. He crowed with delight over the strangeness of the visitors, and touched them here and there with lively curiosity, running his fingertips over the bristling mat of black hair on Brant's burly chest, and fingering the furcaps of the outlaws as if he had never seen such before, which he probably hadn't. He gave

Tuan's stiff tuft of beard a little tug, giggling delightedly. Tuan glowered, but said nothing.

Then the jeweled boy sat down tailor-fashion on a plump peach-colored cushion and clapped his hands. Servants came in from the other partitions of the palace, if that is really what it was, bearing cushions for the newcomers, and they all sat down in a ring and were served candies, jellies, mints and sauces in little ceramic pots, while Azuri chattered with Kirin and Aulli, wanting to hear all about how they had discovered these strange and interesting people.

The palace was a three-story edifice, erected near the center of the raft-city, and seemed to be inhabited by very many people who drifted in and out casually, staring with polite curiosity at the strangers. The walls were hung with sumptuous woven stuffs, littered with gaudy cushions, carpeted luxuriously, and furnished rather skimpily with a few wicker tabourets and stools and little else. Festoons of gauzy, lovely things, resembling silk or paper flowers, hung from the rafters. Since flowers were unknown on the Desert World, Brant decided to himself that they were simply fanciful constructions, wrought from pure imagination. But remembering the tiny white flowers that had starred the indigo moss, he couldn't be sure of this.

Later on, and without even the slightest formality or even bidding Prince Azuri farewell, Aulli and Kirin tugged Brant and Harbin to their feet and led them away to small partitions where they could rest. The boy and girl curled up next to the two men and fell asleep. Brant, who wanted to be alone with his woman, had to comply with the local custom, so he shrugged and stretched out.

"They seem a happy, healthy sort of folk, without sexual inhibitions, like the Polynesians were when the first white explorers found them," Harbin remarked drowsily.

"Yeah," said Brant. "And the explorers taught them to be ashamed of their bodies, to drink whisky, and what syphillis was. I wonder what *we're* going to teach the Sea People?"

The old scientist grimaced at the notion, but made no reply.

* * *

They were simply guests, it turned out, neither captives nor slaves. None of them could have quite expected this, but it was a relief to Brant and an even greater one to that suspicious ruffian, Tuan.

The two found an opportunity to converse privately the next "day," when they met by chance on a gallery-like long balcony on the third floor of the palace. Brant was resting his arms on the rail, looking down to watch nude children of both sexes scrambling about gleefully in tiny boats, pelting each other with handfuls of glowing seawater in some sort of childish game.

"The wise man who walks with Brant, the *Dok-i-tor*, does he know aught of the crystal weapons?" inquired Tuan. Brant confessed lazily that he had not yet had a chance to discuss the matter with Will Harbin. And he countered with a question of his own.

"Is our truce still in force, Tuan?"

"As far as Tuan is concerned, it is. They number a hundred to our one, and armed with those weird weapons, they become formidable as adversaries."

Something else had been on Brant's mind.

"These people are playful, happy, peaceful children," he said. "But we would be very wise to avoid offending them in any way. So, can you keep your men under tight control, Tuan? I mean, keeping their hands off the women and away from the jewels?"

"The band of Tuan will obey to the letter the commands of Tuan," the chieftain said with a vicious gleam in his eye, "or Tuan will—" and here he uttered a gruesome Martian saying that is virtually untranslatable, but had much the same meaning as: "I'll drink their blood with my breakfast cereal."

The two tall men grinned at each other. They were not friends, but were beginning to understand and appreciate the qualities each other possessed, and that is one way of beginning a friendship.

Presently, Tuan drifted away, leaving Brant with his lazy thoughts.

24

The Dream Festival

So it was that the travelers took up lodgings in the palace of Prince Azuri, and it was a rather casual arrangement. In a day or two, Brant arranged things so that he and Zuarra could share one of the cubicles, while Agila and little Suoli found another. Doc Harbin roomed by himself, except when little Aulli shared with him.

As for Tuan, he and the warriors of his band kept strictly to themselves. And, even as the desert chieftain had promised Brant, he did keep his men under tight rein lest they offend the Sea People.

Brant and his companions were free to wander about as they wished, and spent hours exploring the quaint raft-city. Will Harbin was fascinated by the method with which the golden children extracted their glassy metal from the luminous waters of the underground ocean, and reported to Brant—in a rather bewildered fashion—that he simply could not understand how it was managed.

"They pour seawater into huge ceramic urns," he said, and added, puzzled, "*Something* causes the nodules of glassy metal to precipitate on the bottoms of these urns, from which they scrape up the stuff periodically. It comes out in a gummy form, which they then deposit in molds where it hardens, somehow—into metallic form. But don't ask *me* how they do it! Frankly, Jim, I'm wondering if science back Earthside hasn't been wrong all these centuries about alchemy. . . ."

The boy Kirin came by one day to invite Brant on a

"fishing" trip. Zuarra was curious to find out what the lad meant, so they both accompanied the child down to the wharfs, where a merry gang of young people were set to leave.

They had no boats, but something like long fibrous pontoons strapped to their feet, and they moved out to sea by the use of long paddles. Zuarra, to whom the sea was still a fearful and a marvelous thing, decided to stay behind, but watched anxiously as Brant paddled out with the youngsters. He was awkward at maintaining his balance, at which the children hooted and cried, but out of mischief, not from malice.

And suddenly, a swarm of sea-slugs made the surface of the ocean boil. Merrily boasting, the children snagged these with lassoes fastened on the end of short rods, and scooped the wriggling creatures out of the water, tossing them in rattan baskets they wore strapped to their backs. Brant was nowhere near as agile at this as were the youngsters, who had, of course, been accustomed to this form of sport all their young lives.

Brant was curious as to how the children knew where the slugs would rise to the surface, and when. He asked Kirin about this, for by this time he had mastered the local language sufficiently to converse in simple words.

The boy looked puzzled.

"We do not know when they will come, or where," the boy said. "We—*make*—them come."

"How do you do that?" demanded Brant.

Kirin touched his forehead, exactly between and about an inch above his eyes.

"With the *niothya,* of course! How else?"

This word was new to Brant and was not a part of his rudimentary grammar of the tongue of the Sea People. But just about then the fishing got so busy that he decided to explore the matter later, once things had quieted down.

Once the baskets were full, the fishermen returned to Zhah, and Zuarra was heartily relieved to see that Brant had not been harmed by his dreadful exposure to this strange new element called "water."

Later, when Brant told Will Harbin about the enigmatic *niothya*, the old scientist admitted he had never heard of it.

"Sounds like telepathy, to me," he said skeptically. "Another old superstition, long exploded back on Earth. But . . . well, why not? First alchemy, now mind-reading—or mind-control, or whatever. I'll have to start believing in necromancy and black magic next, I suppose!"

As things turned out, that very evening they learned more of this mysterious *niothya* power. Aulli and Kirin came to inform them that they were all invited to a festival, which Prince Azuri was holding in honor of the visitors.

"Sounds all right to me," Brant said amiably. "What sort of a festival is it?" He presumed they had in mind a lot of singing, and dancing, and plenty to eat; but you never could be sure with these lazy, naked people, who entered into amours so casually, and walked away from them at the first signs of boredom.

They might have meant an orgy, and he didn't think Harbin would enjoy that sort of thing.

"Of the *niothya*," the children said in chorus, and left the room. Harbin and Brant exchanged a glance of interest.

"Now perhaps we'll find out what all this mumbojumbo is about," declared the scientist.

That evening they ate in their cubicles, as servants brought succulent dishes on wicker trays to where they all were staying. After the meal, Kirin and Aulli came to fetch them to the festival, and they came to a very large hall which they had not seen before, where rows of benches climbed the walls in tiers, not unlike the bleachers at a sports event.

Taking the places of honor which had been reserved for them, the travelers glanced about curiously, wondering what was about to happen.

"Shall we begin the Festival of Dreams now, O Prince?" inquired one personage who seemed to be acting in the capacity of master of ceremonies on this occasion. Prince Azuri, who was cuddling and whispering with a tall, long-legged girl with pointed breasts like ripe pears, and whom

Brant had been given to understand was the Prince's latest
lover, nodded distractedly.

With an impressive gesture that seemed to command silence,
the master of ceremonies, Hathera, seated himself in the
center of the arena on a plump cushion. Kirin, who sat at
Brant's left, slipped his small hand into the Earthsider's big
paw.

"We must all join hands now," the boy informed him. His
bright eyes were alive with excitement and anticipation. Brant
didn't understand why, but nodded, and took the hand of
Zuarra, who sat at his right. After all, when in Rome. . . .

Silence fell as the throng ceased whispering and chatting.
The quality of the silence was not strained exactly—not one
of breathless suspense—but rather calm, placid, serene. Brant
wondered to himself if they were supposed to pray.

Then Zuarra gasped, and stiffened, and Brant's jaw dropped
in amazement. For out of sheer nothingness formless colors
appeared. Lambent haloes and streamers and shapeless blurs
floated, wound, or drifted. Lilac, pink, cream, orange, lavender,
amber, puce, mauve—it was as if the elves had ransacked a
rainbow for its loveliness, and were invisibly strewing its
luminous treasures on the empty air.

Brant looked around at the nearer faces; all were rapt,
expectant, almost ecstatic. Will Harbin was staring dumb-
founded, his jaw slack. Tuan sat stiffly, bristling with stern
disapproval at this unnatural sorcery. Brant let his gaze return
to the center of the arena, where in mid-air the colors were
still forming.

The luminous hues strengthened, becoming brighter in color
and beginning to shape themselves into definite forms. Some
were things like blossoms, which reminded Brant of the
flowerlike handicrafts which festooned the rafters of the throne
room. Others were like lucent bubbles that floated to and fro.
One such bubble began to chase the others and they fled from
his rush, forming a long train of flying spheres that wound
around the pillars which supported the roof, in and out of the
rafters, causing the younger children to burst into giggling
while the older people watched the lovely game with smiling
faces, nodding judiciously, as if applauding an artistic perform-

ance of some sort. Which was probably exactly what the Festival of Dreams was, after all.

The bolder and more aggressive bubble, unable to catch any of the timid, fleeing ones, paused hovering in the middle of the room and began to blow itself bigger and bigger, as it were. The larger it grew in girth, the fainter became its color—which, by the way, was mauve.

As the tint dimmed, an opalescent display of fleeting shades and admixtures and permutations of color crawled across the surface of the expanding sphere, reminding Brant and Harbin of the wealth of hues sunlight strikes from the oily scum that floats on the surface of water in the gutters of streets.

Zuarra—and many others, too—gave voice to a gasp as the expanding sphere suddenly exploded in a gush of many-colored sparks that fountained into the air and fell back again in curving, graceful streamers. Hers had been a gasp of alarm, however, while the others had gasped at the beauty of the thing.

Like a cloud of fireflies, the shower of sparks collected, formed a whirlpool that slowly revolved, a wheeling vortex formed of minute points of pure light that looked like nothing more than models of the galaxy which Brant had seen back in Nebraska as a boy.

The belt of sparkling light began to revolve faster and faster, sucking up and absorbing all of the other light-shapes in the arena, the floating flowerlike forms, the shapeless blurs, and even the shy bubbles which still lurked or lingered among the rafters of the ceiling.

Now—rousing a concerted murmur of pleasure from the audience—the vortex came apart in long, meandering streamers composed of particles of light. These wove about the room, forming incredible arabesques of sinuous, interweaving complexities that would defy description. Bands of different colors flickered through the weaving spirals in a sequence that began with deepest crimson, then carmine, brick-red, warm pink and so on throughout the spectrum of the colors visible to the human eye, ending in the deepest of violets.

At which point the lights winked out and the show, it seemed, was ended. A thunder of delighted applause crashed like surf upon the head of the master of ceremonies, Hathera, who now could be seen as rather the artist who had orchestrated the display. He bowed deeply, beaming with smiles at the success of his exhibition.

The crowd rose, broke up in groups, and went into adjoining rooms to sample liqueurs from trays already laid out and awaiting them, to discuss among themselves excitedly the quality of the work they had seen.

"That was . . . *niothya*?" asked Brant in an awed whisper of Kirin.

"It was *niothya*," the boy nodded solemnly.

25
The Serpent

They discussed the marvels they had seen later, once the festivities had concluded. The outlaws regarded the phenomenon from the viewpoint of their superstitions.

"It was sorcery—black sorcery—and naught else more!" growled Tuan with truculence and aversion. Will Harbin shook his white head.

"It was a lot more than that," said the older man. "Telepathic communion? A shared illusion, projected into the minds of those in the audience? That fellow Hathera seemed to be in charge somehow, as if he was sharing telepathically his own imaginings. . . ."

"Yeah, but did we *see* what we thought we saw?" demanded Brant.

"Only a camera could give us the answer to that question, Jim," said Harbin. "But I don't think so, not at all. The illusions were projected into our minds, and the visual centers of the brain translated them as floating shapes of color."

"Looked damned real," muttered Brant.

"Remember how we all joined hands?" asked Will Harbin. "Each human body projects a very weak electrical field. And thought itself is electrical in nature, for the brain is, among other things, an electrochemical battery. No, joining hands linked our electrical fields into communion, like they used to do way back in the old days at séances. Hathera then drew upon the communion of minds to conduct a symphony of color-illusions. . . ."

They talked about the thing a bit more, but gave it up as

just another baffling mystery, one of the many Mars concealed in her ancient heart.

Garden of Eden, or Fairyland? Brant wondered: maybe a little of both.

Later on that "night" as they slept, the Serpent at last reared its ugly head.

Brant was sleeping soundly, with Zuarra clasped naked in his arms, when rudely and suddenly roused. Tuan was looming over him, his expression ominous, his eyes cold and dangerous.

"What's up?" growled Brant, coming awake all at once, like a startled jungle thing.

"Is it you, O Brant, have thieved the *f'yagha* weapons from me?" demanded the chieftain, fiercely.

"Which weapons?"

Tuan, in hissing tones, said that the brace of power guns were missing from his side when he awoke. Brant grinned wolfishly, baring strong white teeth.

"You mean the pistols you stole from me, back at the camp?" he inquired sardonically. But Tuan was in a vicious temper, and refused to let the sarcastic implications of Brant's questions faze him in the slightest.

"The same," he snarled. Brant shrugged, opening his arms.

"Look around. See for yourself. I don't have them—didn't take them—and there's nowhere to hide them here."

Without another word, Tuan and his men searched the cubicle, and found no sign of the missing weapons.

"Then who else could have taken them, O Brant, answer that question if you can."

Brant considered. As far as he knew, the Sea People of Zhah still had no idea that the weapons the visitors had borne with them were weapons. Will Harbin would hardly have run the risk of stealing the guns back from Tuan without discussing it first with Brant. And Zuarra had slept all night at his side.

That left only Suoli, who was much too fearful and timid to have risked arousing the ire of the outlaw chief.

Suoli or . . . Agila?

Brant mentioned this to Tuan. The other grunted, turned, stalked stiff-legged from the cubicle.

"Let us go and see," he snapped at Brant over his shoulder.

They went to the cubicle where Agila and Suoli had become accustomed to sleeping, and found it empty. Wild rage flared in the hard eyes of Tuan.

"Tuan should have slain that snake when he had the chance," he muttered to himself between clenched teeth. Brant was about to propose a search of the palace for the missing pair, when the sounds of a distant commotion came to their ears. Cries of consternation and alarm were clearly audible in this many-roomed palace where the very walls were but flimsy screens of woven rattan.

"Come on!" Brant said to Tuan, setting off at a run in the direction from which the startled voices had come.

They pelted along, with Brant and Tuan side by side, and the others hot on their heels, shoving their way through cubicles and suites, rousing bewildered sleepers by their sudden interruption.

Before more than a few minutes had passed, they burst into one of the apartments of Prince Azuri, and stopped short. For they had found the scene of the commotion, and had burst upon a tableau whose nature froze the blood in Brant's veins and raised the hackles on his nape.

"You . . . damned . . . *fool!*" he groaned helplessly. For they were all truly helpless now, and the Serpent had entered into Eden at last. And, which was very much worse, they had brought the Serpent with them, however unknowingly. . . .

Sprawled out stark naked in a jumble of soft, small cushions Prince Azuri lay. Blood ran slowly from a ghastly wound on the side of his head. The travelers could not at once tell whether the young monarch of Zhah was dead or merely unconscious. Then they saw he was not breathing.

The young woman who had been his companion earlier at the Dream Festival now crouched pale and wide-eyed and shivering with fear in the far corner. She seemed merely frightened and shocked, but was unharmed as far as they could tell.

Over the limp body of Prince Azuri, Agila crouched, snarling and showing his white teeth, like a wild beast brought to bay by hunting-hounds. In one hand he clenched one of the two power guns.

From the other hand, looped and trailing chains of jeweled fire flashed and glowed and glimmered. The lean wolf had been in the act of robbing Azuri's body when he had been interrupted.

Zuarra clutched Brant's arm, nodding in the other direction. "Oh, no!" she moaned under her breath. Brant looked in that direction and saw Suoli, shaking with fear or excitement—perhaps from both—holding the other power gun in trembling fingers.

Just before Brant and the others had burst upon the scene of the crime, some of the Sea People who dwelt in the palace had come upon it unexpectedly. It was from their throats had come the cries of alarm and shock and consternation which had alerted Brant and Tuan.

They stood frozen in disbelief, the naked youths and maidens. They seemed not so much angry as appalled, and it occurred to Brant that perhaps never before in their young lives had the Sea People observed a crime of violence. In this peaceful floating paradise, violence and crime, theft and murder, were doubtless completely unknown.

And Brant groaned a curse under his breath, staring at Agila. This dreamlike fairyland, with its innocent golden children had reminded him of the old story of Eden—of Eden before the Serpent. And now the Serpent was come at last into Eden, and they had brought him in. . . .

Agila caught Brant's attention with a savage gesture.

"You speak their strange tongue a little, *f'yagh*," he snarled, his voice shaking as if he was dangerously near to losing his self-control. "Tell them that these things we hold are weapons of great power, weapons that can slay from afar, and of power so great that at will we could bring this city down upon their heads!"

"Agila, don't be more of a fool than you already are,"

said Brant swiftly. "Put down the guns, you and Suoli, and surrender. These are a people given to peaceful ways—at very most, they will drive you out of the city, and the two of you can easily fend for yourselves in the fungus-forests of the mainland—"

The cold, unwinking black eye of his own power gun stabbed in the direction of Brant's gut. "Do as I say," hissed Agila, his eyes wild and wary.

Tuan caught Brant's eye. "Do as the dog orders," whispered the outlaw chief. "Or we are all dead men."

Just then a newcomer came pushing through the shock-frozen crowd of the Sea People, and stopped abruptly at the scene before him. Brant recognized the man as Hathera, he who had orchestrated the Dream Festival earlier, and who seemed in a position of some authority in the palace of Zhah.

Hathera said nothing, not even bothering to inquire what had happened here. He looked sorrowfully at the naked body of his Prince, sprawled in an awkward position like that of a jointed puppet whose strings have suddenly been cut.

"*Aihee!*" moaned Hathera in sobbing tones. "*Aihee*, O my brethren! Behold the young Prince, the beautiful Prince, struck down by the hand of one that was a visitor in his own city and a guest in his own house!" And he swayed, moaning a soft, crooning, wordless song. One by one all of the other Sea People began to sway to the same slow rhythm, joining their voices to his own.

"*Aihee, aihee,*" they chanted. And strangely there was no anger in their expressions, only sadness, a deep, heart-aching sadness that touched Brant to his soul.

"*Aihee*, my brethren, come . . . let us join minds in memory of our fallen Prince, Azuri the Beautiful," moaned Hathera softly, and he closed his eyes as if concentrating, as did all of the Sea People in the room.

And Brant's guts went ice-cold, for he knew exactly what was about to happen—

THE AFTERMATH

26
The Ending

As the Sea People joined hands in mental communion, their eyes became blank and vacant, their faces smoothed from grimaces of sadness and despair into placid expressionlessness.

For a long, breathless moment nothing at all happened.

Then—

Agila staggered, paled to a greenish, sickly hue, his eyes wide and bright with fear and lack of comprehension.

The power gun fell from slackening fingers to thud against the floor-mats.

The thief seemed struggling for breath, face blackening with the effort to suck air into starved lungs. His eyes bulged hideously from their sockets: it was as if bands of iron tightened about his ribs, crushing the breath from him.

Then he fell limply, sprawling across the body of the Prince. He kicked out once or twice, an involuntary action. Then he lay dead as a piece of stone.

And Brant sucked in his breath, heart chill with fear. For he knew exactly what had happened. The communion of minds, it seemed, could touch other nerve centers of the brain besides the visual sense. It could control even the involuntary muscles of the body, those over which the will has little or no control, such as the beating of the heart . . .

The Sea People had slain the murderer of their Prince in their own way . . . by thought alone.

Suoli uttered a shriek of despair when Agila staggered and fell. Now, soft, plump little hands shaking like leaves in a tempest, she turned like a cornered beast upon the folk of Zhah.

Brant's second power gun was in those trembling hands. And Suoli knew how to use it—

"Suoli, *no*—!" the big Earthsider yelled from a raw throat, but she was too far gone in panic even to comprehend his words.

Hathera turned his sorrowful gaze upon the small woman, and she dropped the gun. She sagged and crumpled to the flooring, and crawled feebly some small distance, until her head lay upon the breast of her lover. Then, as if somehow contented, she breathed a small sigh. And . . . died.

An hour or two had passed since that terrible scene in the chambers of the Prince, and Brant paced up and down, restless as a caged tiger. Tuan sat, arms clasped about his knees, face grim, eyes brooding on nothingness.

Strangely enough, no vengeance had been visited upon the rest of the strangers: only upon Agila and Suoli. But the mind-force had herded them together into a side-room, and they found themselves unable to leave it. Doubtless at this very moment Hathera and the leaders of the princely clan were conferring upon the manner of their doom.

The old scientist glanced at Brant impatiently. "Jim, I wish you'd stop pacing back and forth! You're making me nervous."

Brant grunted sourly, and flung himself down beside where Zuarra sat. He said nothing: but all of this waiting was making *him* nervous.

The outlaw chief caught Brant's eye with a small, mirthless grin. "Tuan wishes that the Sea People would make an end to this," he stated flatly. "If they intend to kill us, then by the Timeless Ones, let them get it over with!"

Nobody made reply, but the rest of Tuan's warriors stirred restively, hefting their weapons.

"Maybe we should make a break for it," Brant muttered. "We still have the guns."

"How far would we get?" asked Will Harbin. "Besides,

we can't pass through the door. The mental power of the Sea People holds us under constraint as surely as if there were iron bars across the door."

"We could try *something*," said Brant. "Set the building on fire, maybe. They'd be too busy putting it out to bother with us . . ."

His voice died away lamely into the silence. He knew it was a lousy idea, but the raw instinct to fight for survival was strong within him. Much rather would he go forth to face Death like a man, than crouch like a coward or a weakling, and wait for it to visit him at its leisure. . . .

Suddenly, Will Harbin lifted his head. "Listen!" he whispered. But they had all heard it at the same moment, the distant keening. It was a low, wailing song without words, a moaning as of many voices. And it was coming *nearer*—

Brant and Tuan sprung to their feet, and the others scrambled up upon their cue.

Hathera appeared in the doorway, like a sudden apparition. He was naked, save for a wreath of strange blossoms which crowned his brow. Behind him many others could be seen, men, women, young children. All wore similar wreaths of the curious flowers.

"The time has come for you to leave us," said Hathera softly. His face was lined and weary, his eyes sorrowful, with no animosity in them.

At that moment, the mental constraint which had bound them all within the room—*changed*. They were free to leave the chamber, and a compulsion came upon them to do so. They trooped out into the hallway and Hathera turned, leading them. And, although Tuan's band of outlaws had their weapons ready in their hands, it did not occur to them to use them; perhaps this was another form of the constraint, for by now Hathera had learned the meaning of the word "weapon."

Zuarra slipped her strong, small hand into Brant's, nodding behind them. He looked over his shoulder and saw that the Sea People were bearing the bodies of Agila and Suoli upon stretchers.

The twin power guns lay upon the breasts of the slain couple.

* * *

When they emerged from the central building into the dim luminance of eternal dawn, they saw an unearthly sight.

For all of the people of Zhah, from the oldest man to the babes in their mother's arms, were gathered to observe their passage. In their hundreds and their thousands they stood ranked along the way, and each of them wore the strange crown of blossoms upon their brows.

The soft, sorrowful crooning rose now in a swelling chorus from the throats of many thousands. It was a sad, low susurration, like the sobbing of wind in gaunt boughs, or the sighing of the sea. It raised the hackles on Brant's nape.

He stared into many faces as Hathera led them down to the sea. The same mournful expression was upon each face, and in the eyes of all. Nowhere did he read anger or even resentment: only a stricken, heart-deep sorrow, a hurt puzzlement.

The ship was waiting for them at the end of the long quay, but whether it was the same vessel that had borne them across the luminous sea to the floating city, or another very much resembling it, they could not tell.

They boarded the vessel, and Hathera stood aside to let them pass. Brant felt the urge to say something—to stammer apologies—but the words died in his mouth. There was nothing to say; nothing at all. . . .

The sad-faced children were on board the vessel before them, and the moment the last of the unwelcome visitors strangers had reached the deck, lines were cast off and the captive dragonflies bore the ship away from Zhah.

The elfin city dwindled gradually across the expanse of the shining waters, until it was merely a moat on the horizon. And Brant felt a strange, sad elation rise up within him.

"Guess they're not going to kill us, after all," he muttered to Will Harbin. "Wonder why?"

"God knows," said the older man soberly.

Among the naked children who manned the craft were little Kirin and the girl Aulli who had tutored the two Earthsiders in the ancient tongue of Zhah. But the children only looked at them sadly, wistfully, and did not address the two. Neither did Brant or Harbin attempt to speak to them.

They sat down on the deck, rather shakily, glad to be still alive. A somber mood was upon them all, and they said little to each other, for each was busied with his own thoughts.

The ship sailed on across the glowing sea.

27

Expelled from Eden

The voyage was a dreamlike thing, and ever after they found it difficult to recall aught that occurred during this time. The silent children gave them food and drink; at intervals they slept; when rested, they woke. The children did not address them and left them strictly to themselves.

After a time, the jewel-strewn shore came into view on the horizon, but whether they had been brought back to the same place or not they could not at once discern.

They were put ashore, and the bodies of Suoli and Agila went with them. As he was about to leave the ship, Brant turned and his gaze sought out the face of the boy.

"Kirin," he said awkwardly, but he said no more. For tears welled into the amber eyes of the lad and fell slowly, one by one, down his cheeks. Brant bowed his head and turned away and left.

Once they were all ashore, the ship was turned about and began the voyage back to Zhah. Brant felt a pang go through him as it receded into the haze of the distance.

Will Harbin stood beside him, and they both gazed, rather wistfully, as the ship vanished.

"Can we ever return here again?" murmured the scientist. "The knowledge we could gain, the wisdom, the value to science—!"

Brant said nothing. They both knew that this Eden was forbidden to them, and to all men from the surface world forever. They did not need the vision of the angel with the flaming sword to tell them they were expelled from Eden. . . .

"You have your memories, your notes," Brant said, almost roughly. The old scientist screwed up his face into a rueful expression.

"I do, Jim; but who would ever believe the story, even if he heard it from our own lips?"

Zuarra came toward them, excitement in her face.

"They have returned us to the very place where they found us," she informed them breathlessly. "See? There—our gear and garments—and there! The strange forest where we fed."

She was right, of course. The fungus forest stood as it had always stood, and Brant could even spot the growth from which they had first eaten. Everything was as it had been then . . . the azure moss, with its tiny white star-flowers, the nodding fungi in their rich and varied hues . . . but everything was different.

The weird underground cavern-world had turned against them as swiftly as it had once warmly and innocently welcomed them. And they must soon begone from this enchanted place where they were no longer wanted.

But first there was a grim and melancholy duty to be performed. From his gear, Brant removed an entrenching tool and began to dig the twin graves. When he was winded, one of Tuan's warriors replaced him. They dug the graves shallowly enough, for there were no wolves in this faerie world, no predators who would disturb the peaceful slumbers of the dead.

And they laid to rest Agila and Suoli, wrapped in each other's arms, under the azure moss.

No words were spoken over the dead, for the Martian natives have little in the way of religious ceremonies, as Earthsiders understand the term. If any of them prayed to the Timeless Ones to watch over the slumber of the twain, it was silently and inwardly.

Brant and Zuarra stood side by side, hand clasped in hand, as Tuan's men laid the mossy sod over the dual grave. He stole a sidewise glance at her, and found her face stony and devoid of any expression. Neither were there any tears in her eyes.

She had said her farewells to Suoli long ago, he guessed or knew. . . .

They had buried them without the guns. Those now hung heavy in the hands of Tuan.

The outlaw chief saw that Brant had noticed that he had taken up the power guns that he had once thieved from Brant. Now, his face proud, he approached the Earthsider, who stood easy, empty hands at his side, waiting for whatever might come.

"The truce that was between the people of Brant and the people of Tuan was to last only so long as both were the prisoners of the Sea People," Tuan reminded him softly. Brant nodded.

"I remember."

"It was only right," said Tuan. "Then we were few among very many, outnumbered and alone."

"I know," said Brant levelly.

Suddenly, Tuan did an amazing thing. He extended both hands to Brant, offering the power guns hilt forward. Brant refused to let his surprise show in his face. He accepted the weapons without changing expression, but in his heart he knew. When a warrior of Mars offers a weapon to one of the Hated Ones, it is a gesture of brotherhood, not of friendship: a gesture that means even more than the sharing of water.

Meeting Tuan's eyes squarely, he replaced the guns in their worn holsters.

"He who stole the treasure of my ancestors from me has gone down to death, and paid the expiation for his crime," said Tuan. "Those who were his companions, who remain, are innocent of wrongdoing, for they knew him not at that time, neither did they learn of his crime until later. So be it."

Brant nodded silently. Tuan wet his lips.

"They have been through much together, Tuan and Brant," he declared. "Side by side, they have looked upon wonders such as no man would believe. And never has the one betrayed the other, even when death threatened them all. True has been the trust which Tuan placed in Brant, and truly has that trust been returned. Is it not so?"

"It is so," answered Brant softly.

Tuan grinned. "Then let the truce continue—forever, if needs must! Never shall we be foes again: comrades, if it comes to that—"

"And friends, anyway, if it doesn't," remarked Brant.

They smiled at each other. It was not a Martian custom to shake hands, but the touch was there in their linked eyes.

Tuan turned away, clearing his throat noisily.

"Then let us begone from this place that welcomes us no more," he said gruffly.

Securing their garments and their gear, they found the entrance to the stair again, and paused thereupon for a time, looking off over the strange vista of this weird world, which had become so familiar to them in so brief a span of time.

Zuarra fingered something in the pocket of her robes. She withdrew it and opened her fingers to show Brant the glimmering and jewel-like stone she had taken up from the shores of the luminous sea during the first hours they had spent here in the world of Zhah.

"Zuarra knows in her heart that we are forbidden this place ever again," she said sadly. "But—O, Brant, must I give this stone back to the shores of the sea?"

Brant put his arm around her and grinned down into her wistful, upturned face.

"I think a souvenir is permitted to us," he said gently. The Martian woman said nothing. She replaced the smooth, richly colored gemstone in its pocket, and her expression was radiant.

They stood and gazed for one last time upon the sloping sward of indigo moss, upon the fantastic fungus-forest, and upon the old, gentle hills that hid from their view the luminous waters of the Last Ocean.

Then they turned and began to ascend the stony stair.

28

The Return

The way back up the great stair was harder than before, but, then, this is always the case. It is more difficult to climb a stair than it is to go down one, simply because of gravity.

They carried with them that of their gear and clothing they had abandoned on the indigo moss-slopes. And they climbed— and climbed—with the stronger assisting the weaker of them. From time to time, as before, they paused to rest and refresh themselves on the stone platforms.

It had occurred to them, of course, to take precautions against thirst and hunger. So the outlaws, with their long knives, had carved off slabs of mushroom-meat, and had filled their canteens with sweet fluid from those growths in the fungus-forest which bore the honey-hearted meadlike liquor.

They yearned for fresh water and for cooked meat. But these were not to be had on the stair, and there was naught else for them to do but try to ignore those yearnings which could not then be appeased.

They continued the ascent. After a time, weary, they slept. Only to wake and climb again.

Presently, they began to notice a reversal of the conditions they had observed during their descent of the stair. That is, the wan and pearly luminance slowly ebbed; the humidity seeped from the air and it became dry; the warmth faded, and when, despite the heat of their exertions, it became unpleasantly chill, they paused during one rest-period to don again their garments.

Brant and Will Harbin climbed into their protective, heated

suits of nioflex. The natives, including Zuarra, resumed their long, loose robes. And they climbed up and up, while the air became more like the atmosphere they had known on the surface—cruelly dry, bitterly cold, depleted of all but vestiges of life-giving oxygen.

It was as difficult for their bodies and respiratory systems to readjust to these conditions as it had been earlier. They must pause to rest themselves many times, panting, starved for air, their flesh slick with greasy perspiration as their body-chemistry reverted to the conditions they had known before, on the surface.

In time, they returned to normal.

They spoke little between themselves, saving their breath for the ascent of the stone stair. But during the breaks between the intervals of the ascent, when they rested, drank frugally, ate sparingly of their scant supplies, a few words were exchanged.

Will Harbin's face was screwed into a doleful expression during one such rest period. Brant asked if he was feeling all right; it had occurred to him that the strain on the older man's heart, caused by the long and painful ascent of the stair, might very well prove injurious.

The other shook his head. "My ticker's strong as ever," he declared. "No, I was just mourning the loss to science of the information, the knowledge, the data we could have brought back from Zhah. If only I had brought along a camera! Or specimen-bottles. Incredible or not, my colleagues would have to pay some attention to tissue-samples from the mushroom-trees, or a segment of a dragonfly wing. . . ."

He cast Brant a sour glance, and the big man grinned ruefully, knowing what was in Will Harbin's mind at that moment. He had mightily wished to fill his canteen with water from the luminous sea, but Brant had refused to permit this, on the grounds that they would become mighty thirsty on the stair, and every canteen was needed for nourishing fungus juices.

And, of course, he was quite right. Long before they reached the top of the stair, their supplies of drinkables gave out and their mouths and throats became parched with thirst. But knowing that Brant had been right in refusing him permission made it no easier for the scientist to do without the single water sample which would, if not exactly have proven beyond all doubt or question the existence of the subterranean world beneath the dunes of Mars, at least have surprised and interested the world of science.

He heaved a heavy sigh, and stopped thinking about the loss to human knowledge. Many and strange were the mysteries of Mars, and in all the generations since first the Earthsiders came hither to explore, to colonize, to exploit, few had been uncovered, and multitudes more remained hidden in the hostile wastes of the Red Planet.

Brant's physical powers were amazing to the outlaws, and won him their admiration and respect as nothing had before.

The fact of the matter was very simple. Mars has a gravity far less than that of Earth, where Brant was born and bred. His muscles were shaped to battle against a stronger pull of gravitation, whereas those of the Martian natives were adapted to the lighter gravity of their world.

Nevertheless, his stamina and endurance, his sheer strength alone, made him the object of their admiration. Fighting men from whatever world admire in others the same abilities which they respect in themselves. They found nothing to marvel at in his physical courage, his fighting skills, or his instinct for survival. But his strength and endurance were so far greater than their own—even those lean, tough, rangy desert hawks—that they strove, however in vain, to emulate him.

The grueling toil of the ascent, the bone-deep exhaustion they endured, the oppressive darkness and silence of the stair, was not alleviated by the monotony of the climb.

For there were no surprises on the way back to the surface, only a reversal of the strange—but by now, quite familiar— phenomena they had observed on the earlier journey down.

When there is nothing at all to look at, and even less to

think about, boredom can become as wearisome to the mind as hard physical toil is to the body.

They were by now too parched to talk, or even to sing. There was nothing at all to do but to climb, and climb, and climb, until every muscle and nerve and sinew in their bodies ached beyond that caused by any exertion they had ever known before; and there was nothing to look forward to in hope and anticipation except the next rest stop, and the next morsel of food from their dwindling store.

They all knew that it would eventually end, of course, but when it did, it quite took them by surprise and for a few moments their benumbed minds could not quite register the fact.

Tuan uttered a harsh croaking cry, pointing ahead. They looked, to see the light of Will Harbin's fluoro mirrored in the dull reflective sheen of a huge rectangle of metal.

It was the door that had barred this passageway between two worlds for uncountable hundreds of millennia.

And they had come to the top of the stair at last.

"Thank God," groaned Harbin wearily.

Tuan and his outlaws muttered a ritual phrase in honor of the Timeless Ones—the strange, shadowy gods of the little-known native religion.

Brant said nothing, but relief was visible in his tired, sagging face. He put one arm about Zuarra, whom he had been helping for most of the last hundred steps, and she lay her head against his chest, and her arm crept about his waist.

The wan light of open day glimmered through the rectangle cut from blackness that was the door to the surface world.

29

Comrades

One by one they filed through the open door, wearily depositing the gear they had lugged all this way on the bare floor of the long, narrow cave which led to the cinnamon sands of the desertlands.

Here, heaped against one wall of the cavern, Brant and Harbin and Zuarra found the equipment they had abandoned at the beginning of the descent—the pressure-still, the tents, the bedrolls.

There was still fresh water in the pressure-still, and they all shared it—only a sip or two apiece, but more delicious than any wine they had ever tasted.

"What did you do with our beasts?" Brant asked of the outlaw chief.

"Tethered them with our own steeds in a deep gully not far to the south," Tuan replied. "The men of Tuan salvaged the protective fences that Brant and his comrades abandoned earlier, when they fled by night from their encampment. With these, we rigged a barrier which we hoped would hold at bay whatever predators may roam this far to the south of the world. The gully contained much fodder upon which the beasts could freely feed. With the favor of the Timeless Ones, they should all, or most of them, be strong and fit enough to bear us on the rest of the journey."

Brant nodded. It had come to his notice that Tuan and the other natives—including Zuarra—made more frequent mention of their mysterious gods in speech these past few days.

He grinned inwardly. Could it be that their weird and wonderful adventures in Zhah had given even the savage desert-bandits—religion?

When they were somewhat rested and refreshed, they went to the mouth of the cave and looked out on the familiar scene. Before, the desert wastes had seemed grim and bleak and desolate, but now, somehow, it was like a glimpse of home. They stood and stared for a long time at the gloomy, bruise-purple sky, the small, dull sun, the rolling stretches of the cinnamon sands.

None of them would really miss Zhah, Brant knew with a certainty he could not have explained, even to himself. Not its weird forests or gorgeous flying creatures; not the luminous sea with its shores strewn with opals and nameless gems; not the laughing, naked, golden children or their wonderful floating city.

In time their memories of the subterranean world under the dunes of Mars would lose their freshness and luster, would dim and fade, like half-forgotten dreams.

And in time, perhaps, they would all wonder if their experiences in Zhah had not, after all, been just that: a dream.

From which they must now awake to face the harsher realities of life in the waking world. . . .

Tuan dispatched half of his warriors to see to their riding-beasts, while the remainder searched the cliffside and its gullies and crevices for provender. They were heartily sick of mushroom-meat by now, and craved meat of another sort.

The men returned with the welcome word that the lopers seemingly had not been disturbed, and were all in apparent health and vigor. And before very much more time had passed, the others came back from their hunt, bearing fat lizards, and a good supply of the fat-leafed, bladder-like plants that the pressure-still would convert into fresh, clean water.

That night, under a blaze of unblinking stars, they feasted

magnificently and drank their fill. The outlaws broke into a
low, chanting song that Brant recognized as the victory song
of returning heroes. He grinned somberly enough.

There were no real heroes, he knew. Only survivors.

They slept in the cave, but he and Zuarra shared one of the
tents. It was long since last they had loved together, and he
was as hungry for her body as he had been for meat and
drink.

They woke at the first light of dawn and made ready for
departure. The lopers they saddled, loading their gear and
equipment on the pack-beasts. Brant and Harbin could not
help noticing that none of their possessions had been harmed
or tampered with or plundered. Tuan, when he swore brotherhood even with *f'yagha*, was, it seemed, the soul of honor.

He even returned to Harbin the two laser rifles with which
the scientist and Agila had been armed when first Brant and
the women had encountered them.

When they were in the saddle, Brant guided his beast near
to Tuan's to exchange a few last words.

"Whither, now, will Tuan and his warriors wend their
way?" he inquired, in the polite and formal dialect of the
Tongue.

The outlaw pointed.

"Out into the dustlands, to the edges of that chasm Brant's
people called the Erebus," said the chieftain. "There the
remainder of the warriors of Tuan await his return—unless,
perchance, they have long since given him up for dead, and
wandered off to loot and plunder the fat merchant caravans
farther north!"

They grinned at each other, and then their expressions
sobered. For this was to be the final parting of the ways for
them. And Brant said as much, a trifle awkwardly. The
outlaw chief shrugged carelessly.

"Who knows, O Brant? The world is wide, true, but it is
not wide enough to hold two friends apart for long. Mayhap
we shall even meet again, to ride together, or to face further
marvels. . . ."

His voice trailed away, and he looked thoughtful.

"What is it, Tuan?"

"It is nothing," replied the other, slowly. "But . . . never did Tuan in this life expect to find himself naming one of the *f'yagha* with the name of 'friend.' It is curious how events and happenings can change the hearts of men."

"I know." Brant nodded. "First we were foes, although I knew not why. Then we became allies, facing a common peril. Then comrades. And now, as you say it, friends."

"Friends forever, my brother!" laughed Tuan. "And comrades again, it may come to pass, for who can read the dark and hidden face of future time!"

They sundered their paths, then, Tuan and his outlaws wheeling about and lifting their weapons in the air, raising a mighty shout, a salute to Brant and his party.

"Hai-*yah!*" they thundered, and then, in a storm of fine dust, whirled into the desert and were gone from sight among the sloping, shifting dunes.

Brant and his friends sat their saddles, watching them out of sight.

Will Harbin made a wry grimace. To Brant he observed:

"For a bandit-chief, a wild outlaw, that fellow has the heart of a prince. And with more courtesy and honor than I have observed very often in princes . . ."

"Where do you plan to go now, Doc?" asked Brant, as they left the cave mouth behind and moved at an easy path northward along the base of the cliffs.

"Might as well get back to the trade city of Dakhshan, I guess," said Harbin. "The CA has a commo station there, and I can report to my department that I am alive and well. They'll send a skimmer to pick me up and take me back to Syrtis Port. How about yourself, Jim?"

"No reason why Zuarra and I shouldn't take the long road back to Sun Lake City," said the younger man with a shrug. "The trouble I ran away from has got to have blown over by now, and if the colonials don't like the idea of one of their own marrying a native woman, well, hell, we'll strike off to

some place like Dakhshan, where our two races somehow
manage to live together side by side without fighting. And
I've had enough excitement to last me quite a while . . . I'd
like to settle down like ordinary people, and maybe raise
some kids.''

Zuarra demurely dropped her eyes, smiling in her heart.
And they rode on into the morning, side by side.

Author's Note

This is the fourth, and, probably, the last novel I shall write in a loose sequence of books I think of under the heading of "The Mysteries of Mars." Like the novel in your hands at this moment, all four are set on Colonial Mars about two hundred years from now.

I call these books a sequence, not a series like the five books in my Saga of the Green Star, or the six novels which comprise my Godwane Epic, or the eight which make up the adventures of Jandar of Callisto, because, while each of the other series were linked together by continuing characters and each individual novel was actually one sequence in an overplot, my Martian mysteries are different.

No characters continue from book to book, and no overplot controls them. Actually, the only link of continuity between these four books is that they are laid on the same version of Mars—which was obviously (as the knowledgeable reader, who is an author's bliss, will easily have realized) shaped and influenced to a considerable degree by Leigh Brackett's marvelous series of Martian adventure stories which were published in such science fiction magazines as *Startling Stories* and *Planet* in my early to middle teens.

These yarns had wonderful titles like "Shadow Over Mars" (which Don Wollheim, then at Ace Books, reprinted as *The Sword of Rhinannon*) and "Sea-Kings of Mars," and so on. When I came to create my own version of Mars I was inescapably reminded of hers, and strove to write my novels in something resembling her lean, sinewy prose, which I have always admired and thought excellent.

Whether I have succeeded in capturing much of the Brackettesque prose style is a question I will leave to the reader to answer for himself. . . .

Of the four novels in my Mysteries of Mars sequence, the first to be written (but actually the fourth in chronological order, for reasons which should be perfectly obvious to anyone who has happened to read that first book) was called *The Man Who Loved Mars*. Fawcett Gold Medal published it in 1973. Next came *The Valley Where Time Stood Still*, published in hardcover by Doubleday in 1974 and later in paperback by Pocket Library. The third novel in the sequence, called *The City Outside the World*, was first published in paperback by Berkley Books in 1977.

While the astute reader may well have identified the source and inspiration of these Martian novels as coming from the works of Leigh Brackett (no great secret, since the first of them was dedicated to that lady), many readers may have missed what I was actually doing in this sequence. That is, I was (honest to Ghu!) writing *lost race romances*, and getting away with it somehow, in this day and age, by laying them on Mars a couple of centuries from now, which disguised them as science fiction.

Hardly anybody since the great days of A. Merritt and Edgar Rice Burroughs has been able to get away with writing lost race romances in the vein of H. Rider Haggard *et al*, in the last thirty-five years or so, and I am proud to be the one to do it. Because that variety of fantastic fiction is one of the most fertile, and one that I have always enjoyed the most.

Each of my novels in this sequence has been laid in a different quarter of Mars, and, having now quartered the globe, there is no room left for more.

There are, of course, the twin moons of Mars left . . . and this sequence may not, after all, be finished. But that is for the future, and my publisher, to say.

—Happy Magic!
LIN CARTER

New York, New York, 1983.

Have you discovered DAW's new rising star?

SHARON GREEN

High adventure on alien worlds with women of talent versus men of barbaric determination!

The Terrilian novels

☐ THE WARRIOR WITHIN   (#UE1797—$2.50)
☐ THE WARRIOR
    ENCHAINED   (#UE1789—$2.95)
☐ THE WARRIOR REARMED   (#UE1895—$2.95)

Jalav: Amazon Warrior

☐ THE CRYSTALS OF MIDA   (#UE1735—$2.95)
☐ AN OATH TO MIDA   (#UE1829—$2.95)
☐ CHOSEN OF MIDA   (#UE1927—$2.95)

Readers write: "I have followed with pleasure the Gor series for many years and I can assure you that I am looking forward to Sharon Green's next book."

    "I have always enjoyed John Norman's Gor series but never have I enjoyed a book as much as *The Warrior Within*."

Do you long for the great novels of high adventure such as Edgar Rice Burroughs and Otis Adelbert Kline used to write? You will find them again in these DAW novels, filled with wonder stories of strange worlds and perilous heroics in the grand old-fashioned way:

☐ THE GODS OF XUMA by David J. Lake   (#UE1833—$2.50)
☐ WARLORDS OF XUMA by David J. Lake   (#UE1832—$2.50)
☐ HOME—TO AVALON by Arthur H. Landis (#UE1778—$2.50)
☐ CHEON OF WELTANLAND by Charlotte Stone
                                                    (#UE1877—$2.95)
☐ THE NAPOLEONS OF ERIDANUS by Pierre Barbet
                                                    (#UE1719—$2.25)
☐ THE EMPEROR OF ERIDANUS by Pierre Barbet
                                                    (#UE1860—$2.25)
☐ KIOGA OF THE WILDERNESS by William L. Chester
                                                    (#UE1847—$2.95)
☐ DELIA OF VALLIA by Dray Prescot   (#UE1784—$2.35)
☐ BY THE LIGHT OF THE GREEN STAR by Lin Carter
                                                    (#UE1742—$2.25)
☐ ERIC OF ZANTHODON by Lin Carter   (#UE1731—$2.25)
☐ THE DIAMOND CONTESSA by Kenneth Bulmer
                                                    (#UE1853—$2.50)
☐ THE QUEST FOR CUSH by Charles R. Saunders
                                                    (#UE1909—$2.75)
☐ THE BOOK OF SHAI by Daniel Webster   (#UE1899—$2.25)
